DEFENDING INNOCENCE

DANIELLE STEWART

RANDOM ACTS PUBLISHING

Copyright © 2018 by Danielle Stewart

All rights reserved.

No part of this book may be reproduced in any form or by any electronic or mechanical means, including information storage and retrieval systems, without written permission from the author, except for the use of brief quotations in a book review.

Cover Design by Ginny Gallagher - http://ginsdesigns.com

Stock Photography Credit Attribution Copyright: nata-lunataD/DepositPhotos

❋ Created with Vellum

DEFENDING INNOCENCE

Vera will be a lawyer. Nothing will stop her. Not even the fact that she's from sleepy old Edenville, North Carolina, or the fact that her single father's small business hardly keeps them fed. A lifetime of hard work and perseverance has propelled her to the destiny she's dreamed of. An internship with Edenville's top lawyer, Michael Cooper, might not be glamorous, but staying in the city for the summer wasn't an option. Like always, she'll turn lemons into lemonade. That's easier said than done when Jay shows up to steal her thunder.

Jay has a one-track mind. He's driven to succeed, not out of pride, but desperation. Justice is all he has in mind when he fights his way through law school. Falling for hot-headed Vera is a distraction he can't afford.

When the two collide, seemingly on similar paths, they realize they have nothing in common but their chosen professional goals. When a cut and dry conviction becomes their summer project, Jay and Vera need each other if they plan to win. Even more if they want to stay alive.

PROLOGUE

Jay

I laugh when I hear someone say: *I'm no expert* then proceed to give you an earful on the topic as if they were. People have been giving me advice my entire life. Completely unsolicited. When I was younger I had that look about me. A kind person would have called me a free spirit. The judgmental sort would be quick to shove me into the box of a radical nonconformist. A beatnik. A wandering soul anchored to nothing. Then I started law school. Nothing solidifies your status as one of the herd like a necktie, a stack of law books, and crippling school debt. But it will all be worth it someday.

I don't let the outside world dictate my life. That hippy-dippy spirit is still a part of who I am. I take the tests. I read the literature. I check off all the boxes, but at the end of the day, I'm Jay Crowley, and I make the world work for me, not the other way around.

My father always said seconds are expensive and non-refundable, spend them wisely. It's time to start cashing mine in for something worthwhile. And maybe that's exactly what will be waiting for me in Edenville.

CHAPTER 1

"When do I ever ask you for anything?" Betty stood with a hand propped up on her hip and one eyebrow raised high. Michael couldn't help but chuckle.

"I'm literally taking out your trash right now. You just asked me to do that." She huffed and followed him out to the porch as he lifted the heavy bags into the barrel by the bushes.

"That is not a favor; that is a transaction. I fed you and your family, and now you take out the trash. This is different." He already knew he had lost this battle. His mother-in-law had that look in her eyes. That little flash of lightning she so kindly handed down to her daughter. Jules could brew the same storm in her eyes when she didn't intend to back down. He loved that about his mother-in-law and his wife most days, but today was a Wednesday, the middle of a long workweek, and he was tired. Her request was only going to complicate things for him.

"I already have an intern coming. It's Vera, Rob Pedro's daughter. You adore her."

"I do." Betty nodded, and followed him back into the kitchen. "I'm sure she and Jay can get on just fine. Interns are free labor, I don't know why you're complaining."

"Our firm is very small. I need half an intern most weeks. Now I'm going to have two. There isn't enough work for them. Vera has been begging me for six years to take her on as an intern when she was ready at law school. She's finally there, and now I'm going to tell her I have two interns and not enough to do."

"You'll find work for them. You're good like that."

"Now comes the empty flattery."

"Is it working?" Betty smiled sweetly as she handed him a towel to dry the dishes. Everyone else had finished Wednesday night dinner and settled out back around the fire Bobby had built. The summer had started slowly, the nights still cooler than usual. He could hear the laughter bubbling up from the backyard. He was going to lose this argument anyway, at least if he fell on his sword now he could still get a marshmallow.

"How do you even know this kid?"

"His great aunt Tabby and I went to high school here together. You know all the stuff that was going on in Edenville in those days. She was a good friend to me and Stan when things were especially hard. She moved to South Carolina after school, but we kept in touch. Jay is in law school, and he needs some direction. A mentor."

"What year of law school is he in?"

"I don't know."

"What school is he going to?"

"No clue."

"What do you know?"

"His GPA is basically a decimal point. She's worried about him and last time we talked she asked if you'd take him under your wing. He's sweet as pie. I met him when he was four years old, and I'll tell you, he's a darling."

Michael considered poking holes in her argument as to the boy's sweetness, considering that was probably twenty or more years ago. Not only was he getting an extra intern, the kid was basically flunking out of law school. Not what he needed right now. But there was that marshmallow to consider. The smell of cedar wood burning filled his nose through the open kitchen windows. Did Jules bring everything for s'mores? Probably.

"Fine, I'll figure something out for both of them. But I can't commit to being any kind of mentor. I'll give them both some hands-on experience, but it's mostly grunt work. It's a lot of making photocopies and running around. If he's about to take the bar exam I can't be his tutor."

"That's not why she sent him here," Betty said, lighting with excitement. "I'll even let you off dish duty." She pulled the drying towel out of his hands.

"She sent him here? He's already here?"

"No," Betty said, waving him off, "he lands in an hour."

"So asking me was more of a formality."

She fluttered her lashes. "It seems so."

"Well fine. I'm going out to the fire. Want me to bring you a chair?"

"You won't have time." Betty looked down at her watch and creased her brow.

"Time for what?"

"To get him from the airport."

"I'm picking him up?" Michael drew in a sharp breath. "He can't rent a car or catch a cab?"

"Funds are tight."

"And he'll be working for free? How is he swinging that? Or am I throwing in a paycheck and a 401K?"

"Well if you . . ."

"Betty."

"He's staying here with us. Borrowing our car. He's going to bus tables at the Wise Owl whenever he's not working for you. That'll give him enough money to get by. He just needs a ride here from the airport, that's all."

Michael took his keys off the large metal hook at the door. "You are lucky you made such a damn good dinner tonight. I should have known something was up when it was all my favorite things. Was that nutmeg in the mac and cheese?"

"I know you like it like that." She winked and then pulled him in for a hug. "You're a good man, Michael. My daughter and grandkids could not have asked for a better guy. That's not empty flattery anymore. It's the real stuff."

"Next time I'm stuck in a tricky case, I'm going to have you do the cross examination. You could sell matches to the devil himself."

"No," she said, modestly waving him off. "Speaking of matches, can you pick up some milk on the way back here? We're out."

"How do matches have any—?" He shook his head and saved himself the next five minutes of a debate. "Whole milk?"

"Yes dear."

"Any surprises I need to know about with this kid?"

"Well if there was, I certainly wouldn't be one to spoil a surprise."

CHAPTER 2

"You look sort of pissed." The tension in the car was thick and although Jay was usually comfortable in any new situation, this was awkward as hell. Michael was a tall, well-dressed guy you could tell was a dad from a mile away. He had that salt and pepper hair at his temples and that crease in his brow from worry. Jay wasn't sure if his presence was making that crease deeper than usual.

"I'm not."

"Oh good," Jay chuckled, "so you always grip the steering wheel that tight and grind your teeth?"

Michael cracked a small smile. "It would suck for you if I did."

"Yeah, a long summer working for an angry guy."

"I'll be honest, I didn't sign up for this. Betty likes to pull the strings and we're all her puppets." He moved one arm like a marionette and rolled his eyes.

"My aunt loves her. She talks about Betty like she's some kind of patron saint. I figured you must be too if you agreed to take a guy like me on as your intern over the summer. No other firm would give me a second look."

"Agree is a bit of a misnomer. You know when a gator grabs its prey and then goes into that death spiral? That's how Betty convinced me to take you on."

"Oh." Jay felt the knot in his stomach yank tighter. "Well it's not too late to put me on a bus and send me the rest of the way to South Carolina."

"I could." Michael chewed on his lip as though he were considering it. "But I can't imagine that putting up with you for a summer could possibly be worse than going another round with the gator."

"Good point."

"What's the deal with your grades anyway? Too much partying? Slacking off?"

"I guess." Jay shrugged. He hated to lie to the guy. He seemed nice enough. But there was a time and place for honesty and this wasn't it. "I'll get back on track. I'm sure you'll inspire me this summer."

Michael held up his hand, his palm down. "This is the bar that represents me inspiring you." He lowered his hand dramatically. "I'm going to need you to put your expectations somewhere around here instead. Maybe we can settle for me teaching you how to unjam the photocopier and restock the toilet paper in the bathroom."

"That's fine too. I can take orders and go with the flow. I'm easygoing."

"Well then, we found it." Michael slapped the steering wheel in a eureka moment.

"Found what?"

"The problem with your grades. Lawyers are a lot of things, but I've yet to meet one that's easygoing. The most common traits are usually overachieving and stubborn, with a healthy dose of narcissism. You might be too well balanced to be a lawyer. Have you thought of a career in guided meditation?"

"I'm in law school. I'll try to be more of a dogged debater and conceited jerk over the summer. For now though, I'm happy to have a chance to learn from an expert. Betty really talked you up. She says you're a hotshot lawyer."

"It's impossible to be one of those in Edenville. Most days I'm settling disputes about grazing lands and bar fights. Actually, come to think of it, if you want to learn anything you should watch Betty. I wonder if she's taking on interns?"

"I'm sure it's not that bad. She's like a little old lady, right? My great aunt just plays cards and does needlepoint. I assumed Betty was the same." Jay watched as Michael animatedly swiped at his turn signal and turned into the parking lot of the supermarket.

"I'm about to buy her a gallon of milk on my way home from picking up a stranger at the airport for her. That little old lady is a mental ninja. I can teach you how to file a case report. She can teach you how to run the world."

CHAPTER 3

Breakfast more than made up for the crick in his neck. Jay didn't care that the bed in Betty's spare room was older than he was and tiny as hell. His legs hung over the edge and stuck out from under the pink frilly blanket. It had been Betty's daughter's room and seemingly remained unchanged over the decades. But it was free. That was what this endeavor required.

All his discomfort was forgotten the second the fluffy stack of pancakes hit his plate.

"You better eat up. Michael hardly ever stops for lunch. Bacon or sausage?"

Before Jay could answer, Betty put two of each on his plate. "Are you sure it's no trouble having me here? I really appreciate the place to stay and the car."

"Clay and I always drive to the restaurant together anyway. My car just sits around. It's good to get it running every now and then. We're happy to have you."

"I'm grateful, and so is my aunt."

"I owe her one, so this is good for my soul."

"Why do you owe her one?" Jay chuckled as he considered

what kind of debt Betty could have racked up with his aunt. She was one of those women who had been old his whole life. He couldn't picture her doing much for anyone.

"When we were in school there were tough times around these parts. The civil rights movement was bursting to life and fault lines were being drawn. Stan and I weren't always popular for our views, but your great aunt Tabby was a true friend. Tough as nails."

"Tabby? Really? She's always been so frail. It's hard to believe you two are even the same age." Jay took a sip of the ice-cold orange juice and tried to imagine his little aunt the way Betty was describing.

"Well she took sick before you were born and look at her, she's still fighting today. Impressive woman."

"She says the same about you."

"And what do people say about you?" Betty locked eyes on him and pursed her lips. "I've gone out on a limb for you here. Michael is doing you quite the favor. I expect you'll afford him the proper respect?"

"Of course." Jay instinctively sat up straighter. "I know it might seem like I'm a screwup because of my grades. That's not it at all. I really appreciate what you've done, and I'll make sure anything I do reflects well on Michael."

Her face softened as she slipped her apron off. "Attaboy. Now hurry up and eat. You don't want to be late on your first day. I'm going to go out in the garden for a bit. There's a lunch in the brown bag on the counter. Take a few of those muffins in for the office to share."

"You didn't have to do that." Jay's chest flooded with affection. No one had ever packed him a lunch before. He'd always bought at school and been a little envious of the kids next to him with their homemade, cut-in-half sandwiches.

"The best parts of life are made up of things we don't have to do, but we do anyway." Like a fallen leaf on a breeze, she whisked out the front screen door. Jay sat in front of his breakfast in the small quiet kitchen and wondered if he was doing the right thing. He'd thought by his mid-twenties he'd be able to walk into most situations and answer that question. But uncertainty seemed to be the only certain thing in life.

Trying to be the best guest he could, he washed his breakfast dishes, wiped down the table, and grabbed the keys to Betty's car.

"You have your lunch?" Betty asked as she wiped her garden glove across her forehead. She was kneeling in the flowerbed with a small stack of weeds by her side.

"Yes." Jay held up the brown paper bag and smiled. "I'll see you tonight."

"Jay, remember dear, grades are only a part of who you are. Your aunt spoke so highly of your character. That lives on long past school marks."

He couldn't muster even a thank you. He just nodded and fumbled with the keys. He'd gotten himself through life. Independence didn't bother him, but maybe that was only because he didn't realize what it would be like to have someone like Betty around.

The ride to Michael's office reminded him just how much he missed being home. Law school in Connecticut was interesting and different, but it wasn't home. Dillon Port, South Carolina was a coastal town full of old slanted houses and even older trees. Unlike most of the towns around it, Dillon hadn't been flooded with summer tourists or builders looking to put up condos. Mostly because it was flooded with something else. Water. It was a low-lying swampy kind of place, and that kept the summer traffic from coming in. It also kept progress from happening.

Edenville had the throwback vibe too. There was a sense of being untouched by the future. Slow pace. Winding roads. It gave him a small sense of peace. That feeling quickly evaporated as he walked through the glass doors to the lobby of Michael's office.

"Can I help you?" A petite woman with wild curls eyed him curiously. She had fresh lip gloss, stunning dark eyes, and a business suit that made her look a little like she was dressing up in her mother's clothes.

"I'm Jay, Michael Cooper's intern for the summer."

"No."

"No?"

"You're mistaken. I'm the intern here this summer." She leaned back slightly and raked her eyes over him. Jay wasn't in a suit, but he had put on his best shirt and dress pants, though they were a bit wrinkled from his suitcase.

"We both are." He looked over her shoulder, hoping Michael would come out and rescue him. "Is he here yet?"

"No, he gets in at nine. I came at eight to make sure there was fresh coffee and the office was tidy. I also checked the voicemail so he'd be ready to return messages when he arrived."

"Oh," Jay said, clearing his throat. "I brought muffins."

She narrowed her eyes. "Leave the muffins when you go."

"I'm not going. Michael can explain. I'm going to be interning here too."

"He's never had two interns. I've lived here my whole life and from the moment I knew I was going to law school I have reserved my spot as an intern here. Who are you anyway and why pick this law firm?"

"I couldn't get in anywhere else. My grades suck."

"Well mine don't. I have a 4.1 GPA at NYU."

"Then why come back here? There are dozens of amazing law firms in New York that would be better choices for an internship." He put the muffins and his lunch bag on the counter, took his laptop bag off his shoulder, and laid it down. All indicating he was staying.

"Because my scholarships barely cover my tuition. I pay my own room and board with the money I make from the coffee shop where I work thirty hours a week. I can't afford to work for free at a law firm in the city and pay for a place to stay. When I'm back here at home I can work doing inventory and accounting for my dad's auto parts store at night and on the weekends. That is why I'm here." She tilted her head to the side and waited for his rebuttal. *Damn she'd be a good lawyer.* Much better than he would.

"I'm going to be paying back school loans until I'm eighty-seven years old." Jay waited to see if her plump pink lips would curl into a smile. They didn't.

"Oh good," Michael groaned as he strolled in and eyed them. "You're both here. How fun."

"Since when do you have two interns?" She practically shoved Jay out of the way to plead her case to Michael. "The caseload here is already so light. There's nothing remotely exciting for one person to do. If we have to split the work between two people, there won't be anything to do. I'm planning on putting this on my applications for the real law firms where I want to intern next year when I have money saved up to stay in the city in the summer. They'll already be skeptical. If they see I couldn't do this job on my own, they'll never take me."

Michael smiled and walked toward his office, and they both obediently followed. "I'm going to ignore the fact that you implied this isn't a real law firm and that nothing exciting happens here."

"Come on, it's all divorces and drunk and disorderly charges." Michael laughed.

"This isn't funny." She propped her fists up on her hips. "Tell him the position has been filled."

"Jay the position has been filled. Vera here is my intern." Michael nodded and folded his arms over his chest. "I'll just need you to pretend to come here every day and tell Betty it's going great."

"Betty?" Vera's face fell slightly. "She's making you do this?"

"Yup." Michael shrugged and took a seat behind his desk. "She insisted. Wouldn't take no for an answer."

"Oh." Vera licked her lips and was clearly trying to search her brain for a solution. "I didn't know that."

"That's it?" Jay looked at both of them in astonishment. "You're giving up that easy? I thought for sure you'd toss me out of here with your own two hands."

She narrowed her eyes at him. "I bet you'd like that."

Michael thumbed through the messages that Vera handed him. "We're not getting out of this, Vera. I say we make the best of it."

"How? He and I switch off making coffee every day?"

Jay knew the time was finally right. "We could dig into an old case. I've done some work with the Justice and Freedom Project. Vera and I could pull an old case, maybe see if we could dig up something new." He tried not to look to eager or give himself away.

Michael leaned back in his chair and considered it. "Our firm does pro bono work a few times a year. Mostly we dedicate time to doing legal work for charities and non-profits. The right case could keep you two very busy."

"You're going to let us work on a cold case?" Vera lit with excitement.

Michael rubbed his chin. "Pitch me a case tomorrow and we'll see. I even have a good friend in New York who does this kind of thing for a living. I may let you use Willow as a resource."

"What's the criteria? Parameters?" Vera grabbed a pen from Michael's desk and pulled a notebook from her pocket.

Michael laughed. "This isn't a class, Vera. No grade. I haven't said yes yet. Whatever you two do will be a reflection on this firm and me. I can't have you out there like a couple of bulls in a china shop. If a case was easy to crack someone besides you would have done it by now. I think we should look at whatever you pick like a learning experience, not something to feed your hero complex."

Jay cleared his throat. "We can do that."

"All right." Michael tossed his hands up as though he were giving in. "You two do some work around the office today and find a case. Pitch it to me tomorrow. Make sure you've thought it through. If I shoot it down, you might not get another chance. I'll be returning phone calls this morning, and then I have to be in court for the afternoon."

"I'll go to court with you." Vera shot her hand up like an anxious fourth grader hoping to be picked to write on the board.

"I would take you," Michael began, "but I want you to learn a valuable lesson. You see, lawyers are egomaniacs. Completely fragile. No matter how well you know them, it's dangerous for your career to insult them."

"Like I did a few minutes ago." Vera sighed sheepishly.

"Right. So your lesson for today is that instead of coming to court with me you'll be refilling staplers and sorting paper clips. It'll give you both plenty of time to figure out what to pitch to me tomorrow."

Vera slumped her thin shoulders and edged out of the office like a puppy who'd been scolded for the first time.

"That was your fault," she hissed as they made their way to the small conference room where they'd be doing their work.

"How was that my fault?" Jay asked, completely enamored with this odd woman. "You're the one who called this place dull."

"You showing up here threw me off my game. I don't like surprises. I had this whole summer planned. I was going to actually shadow Michael and learn something real. It's supposed to be predictable not all crazy like this."

"Who ever told you that?" Jay laughed but stopped abruptly when he realized how wounded she seemed.

"There are things you can do to make your life go a certain way. I'm proof of that. A first-generation kid whose family lives paycheck to paycheck puts herself through law school. I was raised by a single father. Being brown in Edenville isn't always easy either. My point is I'm in control of changing my circumstances, and you're messing with a part of the plan." Vera picked up a stack of mail and started opening it with much more force than it required.

"You can't orchestrate life. If you could people would be doing a hell of a lot better. I think it's great that you're a badass woman with a dogged determination to change her circumstances. But not everything is in your control."

She narrowed her eyes at him and shook her head. "I'm going to pick a case tomorrow that's going to change the game. It'll get published in some law review. If Michael really connects me with a contact in New York, there is hope I can salvage this summer."

"We."

"We what?"

"We are going to pick a case. That's what Michael said. I've done some work like this before. You're only in your first year of law school. I have more experience than you." He shouldn't have gotten quite so much pleasure out of the anger that flashed on her face. But when her nostrils flared and her eyes flamed he couldn't help but smile. On the inside that is.

"It sounded more like you are failing out of law school. Are you even remotely ready to take the bar? Do you have a single prospect for a job once you do? Time spent wandering through school and barely passing does not equate to more experience. Now if you're talking about a beer funnel and frat parties then yes, I'm sure you're a pro."

"You know you might be on the wrong path. You sound a lot

more like a judge than a lawyer." Jay sat at the table and opened his laptop. Vera hadn't been a part of his own plan this summer. She wouldn't be easily convinced of anything, and she certainly wouldn't put up with any of his nonsense. As she tucked her wild curls back behind her ears and sorted the mail he realized something even more concerning. It would be hard as hell to stop staring at her and get any work done at all.

CHAPTER 4

"We are not leaving here tonight until you agree with me." Vera held her pen so tightly the plastic made a small crackling noise under her grip. Jay was infuriating. From his shaggy hair to the way he sat back casually in the chair across from her. In her wildest dreams she couldn't picture this man in a courtroom except maybe as a defendant.

"Is this turning into a hostage situation?" Jay flashed that silly little smile that drove her mad. Could he not be serious about anything? "I don't mind. I just want to make sure we have snacks. Should I go back to the vending machine?"

"Why are you making this so hard? Do you like making me crazy?" Vera watched as his eyes darted away. Another reason this guy couldn't make it as a lawyer. No poker face. "Well I'm not here for your entertainment. Can you please just agree to one of these two cases I've picked out? They are perfect."

"They aren't." He stood and circled the room, doing a lap around the conference room table. "But you don't want my opinion; you've made that clear. Something tells me you don't respond well to criticism."

She pursed her lips and nearly admitted he was right. But that was not happening. "These cases are perfect. They are relevant. Captivating. People will be interested in them."

"What does that have to do with anything? We're talking about working to exonerate someone who might have been wrongfully convicted. We're talking about seeking real justice in a broken system." For the first time since they'd met, Jay seemed to show some actual conviction and passion about a topic. He was wrong, but at least he was being real.

She sat on the edge of the conference room table and readied for another argument. They'd been at it all day, and as infuriating as he was, she had to admit he could at least keep up with the banter between them. "Who goes to law school with the opinion the legal system is broken? We're supposed to be starry-eyed and optimistic, certain we can be a part of what makes this country great."

"You feel that way?" He leaned against the wall and folded his arms across his chest. "You know the incarceration rates in this country. You know how we compare to the rest of the world. And look at us right now, going through dozens of cases that were likely wrong convictions. How can you say our system isn't broken?"

Michael tapped on the door and leaned in. "What are you two still doing here?"

"Apparently we're debating whether or not rule of law matters and if our society should just practice martial law or anarchy." She sipped her iced coffee and smirked.

"So still getting to know each other, I see." Michael put his briefcase on the table and took a seat. Vera assumed he'd want to get out of there, but he had a curious look on his face. That, she believed, was what made a good lawyer. A person who couldn't walk away from a moment like this.

"I wasn't arguing for anarchy." Jay shook his head. "The system can be critically flawed and still be better than nothing."

"Is that how people in school describe you?" Vera was quick. She could zing someone before they saw it coming. It made keeping friends hard. But who had time for friends anyway?

"Low blow." Michael laughed. "Listen you aren't going to solve this tonight. If you want my two cents, I agree the system is flawed. Some days I'd even call it broken. But that's why I do what I do." He looked over at Vera and smirked. "As boring as it might seem some days, even law in a little town like Edenville matters. Those divorces and land disputes matter. And trust me, I wish I could call my life boring, but my family and friends continue to make sure I get sucked into all sorts of drama and danger. But I must be a glutton for punishment because here I am, telling you two to start digging into some old case. Did you find one?"

"Yes," Vera answered eagerly. "Two actually. We were just narrowing it down."

"She hasn't even heard about the case I'm suggesting," Jay interrupted. "Law school 101: get all the facts first."

"Did you pass law school 101?"

"Kids," Michael called, raising his hands. "As fun as this is to watch, I think we should give you something more productive to put your obviously pent-up energy into. Let's hear your cases, I'll decide."

"I have two," Vera said anxiously.

"Pick the best one."

"I thought we'd have until tomorrow." She cleared her throat nervously. More surprises. Didn't these people know how much she hated the unexpected?

Michael's face softened as he morphed into dad mode. "You can do this, Vera. Pick which one you think is the best and lay it on me."

"All right." She shuffled the papers around and tried to make the best of the situation. "Jason Borke was convicted of murder in 1995. He's been in prison serving a life sentence in New York ever since. He's maintained his innocence and says that DNA evidence would exonerate him. But the backlog of testing has kept him from being able to prove that."

"Does he have an alibi?" Michael leaned in. "Have you read the case files?"

"Not all of them. He didn't have an alibi."

"Motive?"

"Well apparently he'd been arguing with the victim earlier that day."

"So we'd be solely relying on getting DNA tested in order to prove his innocence. What kind of DNA do they have?"

"There was blood not belonging to the victim at the scene and on his clothes. It did match the defendant's blood type, but we know that isn't enough."

"Do you think that finding out the blood is not his will be enough to overturn a solid conviction? Couldn't it be argued that the blood might not belong to his killer but to someone else? From some other time or incident."

"I mean it could but . . ."

"You'd need to read the case file thoroughly and look for other evidence that could support his innocence. Something that wasn't presented in court. DNA isn't the magic bullet everyone makes it out to be. In some cases like sexual assault it can be more compelling. I'm not saying this case doesn't have some potential, but it's not a slam dunk by any means."

Vera could only nod as she tucked her papers away. "I can do some more reading tonight."

"Let's hear what you have, Jay."

"Mary-Lee Stevens." He opened the file and launched right

in. "In 1993 she was convicted of murdering her son, nine-month-old Pauly Stevens."

"Filicide?" Vera called out with a laugh. "Are you joking? You think people are going to want to see a convicted mother who killed her child be set free?"

Jay straightened his back. "We're not talking about the court of public opinion. We're talking about the actual justice system."

Michael tilted his head to the side curiously. "Let's hear him out."

"From what I read this afternoon, the trial was fast and weak. There were no character witnesses called on her behalf at all. Not one person testified to what kind of mother she was, or if there had ever been a history of abuse or neglect."

"An oversight." Michael shrugged but wasn't convinced. "Certainly not cause to overturn a conviction or even grant a retrial. The defense might not have been able to find anyone willing to speak on her behalf."

"The jury was biased by the climate at the time. Six other prominent cases of filicide were in the news. Women with postpartum depression were drowning their kids in the tub or driving their cars off cliffs. It was something that had hardly been seen before and was now on the cover of every newspaper."

"Also interesting, but not enough."

"The medical witnesses called, from the testimony I read today, were far from experts. They were talking far more about emotional drives of mothers who kill their children than anything specific to Mary-Lee. Testimony was sensationalized and not at all rooted in fact. Two went on to write books about the case and made six-figure payouts on it."

"Slimy but still not compelling enough to overturn a conviction. What makes you believe she's innocent?"

"I don't have any idea if she's innocent," Jay corrected confidently. "But I don't believe she received a fair trial. The science has evolved over the couple decades she's been in prison. They believe she was poisoning her son. It's not exactly the same situation, but look at how much more we know about shaken baby syndrome. Dozens of people went to prison before scientists understood the condition better. It wasn't always about the last person with the baby. The effects could be slow and cumulative."

"She may have poisoned her baby to death," Vera said, her stomach turning with anger—the same way most anyone would feel upon hearing the circumstances.

"She may have." Jay closed the folder and tossed it on the table. "But she may not have. Then she's only a woman who lost her child and spent years in prison for something she didn't do."

Michael had a big grin on his face as he took the folder and started thumbing through. "It won't be sexy. It won't be popular. There probably won't be a smoking gun. DNA won't come into play. We'd essentially be challenging whether the prosecution did their job, not whether she is innocent."

Vera shook her head. "Those all sound like reasons not to do it."

"Michael, would we have really had resources to test DNA anyway?"

"Not a chance."

"Then at least with this case we can do one of the most basic and free things available. We can talk to people. We can interview people familiar with the family. We can see where the science is today. The case is in South Carolina. We'd have access."

Michael rubbed his hand over the five o'clock shadow on his chin. "What are the three basic ways to get a new trial?"

Vera raised her hand and then put it down suddenly, her cheeks pink. She was built for the classroom; it was real life where she was awkward as hell. "Fixing a legal error, discovery of new evidence, or correcting an injustice like finding the jury wasn't truly impartial."

"So that would be your burden. If you could drum up something solid to meet that criteria I'd get the right people involved and see what we could do."

"If you let me pitch the second case I was looking at, " Vera's voice raised with urgency, "I really think we could approach this with better odds."

"Sorry kid," Michael said as he stood and pushed the chair back in to the conference room table. "My mind is made up and dinner is waiting for me at home. You two need to work together on this. You won't get anywhere if you're spinning your tires in different directions. You don't see it yet, but you both bring something different to the table, and if you're serious about this, you should be willing to do whatever it takes. Even putting up with each other."

"That is a lot to ask." Jay kept his face serious as he eyed Vera.

Vera bit at the inside of her lip until she tasted blood and didn't say a word. She wouldn't give him the satisfaction. She'd been a brat to Michael earlier and maybe she was still paying for it. If there was one lesson her father taught her, it was if you're already standing in a hole, stop digging.

"I'm locking up now. Come on you two. Vera, you need a ride back to your place?" Michael fished out the keys to the office and headed to the door.

"I'll give you a ride," Jay said, clearly still glowing from his victory.

"Good. Jules is already calling me to see where I am. Thanks." Michael waved them off as they headed to parking lot.

"Who says I want to get in a car with you?" Vera stood, boiling in her anger. She was mad at him for winning. Mad at herself for losing.

"You want to ride on the roof?" He opened her car door and waited for her to sit.

"Why are you doing that?"

"What?"

"Opening my door?"

"Do they do things different here in North Carolina? Do the girls climb in the windows or something?"

She rolled her eyes and sank into the front seat reluctantly. "You don't need to open my car door."

"I know." He slid into the driver seat and turned the engine. It didn't start.

Click. Click. Click.

"Are you serious?" Vera leaned in so she could watch him try to turn the engine over as if he might be doing it wrong.

"The battery?"

"No, it's not the battery." She pointed at the icon on the dash indicating it was fully charged. "It's the starter. I need a rock."

"Are you going to hit me with it?"

"I'd like to, but the only thing I want more is to get home." She turned the flashlight on her phone on and hunted the edge of the parking lot.

"Can't we just call a tow truck?"

"We could, but do you know who drives the tow truck in Edenville? My dad. You feel like meeting my dad right now? He will not appreciate coming out here for this. Oh here." She picked up a rock the size of her palm and made her way back to the car.

"What are you doing?"

"I'm going to hit the starter with this rock."

"Why?"

"Because I don't have a hammer."

"Ah, okay?"

She slid on her back on the pavement and heard Jay let out a nervous breath.

"Are you all right?" he asked, crouching down to see better.

"I'm going to hit the starter with this rock and then you're going to crank the engine. We'll drive it to my dad's shop. You need a starter. You can borrow one of his trucks to get back to Betty's tonight."

"How do you know how to do that?"

"Necessity. You'd be amazed how many crappy cars we've had over the years. This isn't a long-term solution, but it'll get us back to my dad's place. I've worked on cars with him for as long as I can remember. Now start it up."

She slid out from under the car and dusted herself off as the engine groaned pitifully to life. As she sat back in the passenger seat she didn't dare look over at his expression. She didn't need to; she could feel his impressed eyes locked in on her.

"That was so hot." He put the car in drive and she rolled her eyes. "You are a badass."

"I'm always here for a damsel in distress." When he laughed the butterflies in her stomach erupted. It killed her to care what he thought. It drove her mad to react at all to him. "My dad's shop is down a couple miles on the right. You can't miss it. There's a huge flashing neon sign that says Pedro's Automotive."

"Sorry about this. I borrowed this car from Betty. I didn't realize it would need a starter. If your dad replaces it I'll pay him for it. It's the least I can do for Betty putting me up in her house and lending the car to me."

"She's not going to let you do that, and for that matter once my dad sees it's Betty's car, he won't take his payment in anything besides free fried chicken at her restaurant every Tuesday night for a month."

"You can't get that kind of service in New York."

"You can get anything you want in the city," Vera corrected. "You can fall in love. You can break a heart. You can stand on the tallest skyscraper or ride in a tunnel beneath the streets. Every corner has a different kind of food. Every store has things you can't find anywhere else in the world. Edenville is a small corner store and New York is a high-fashion mall."

"Don't you get homesick? Living in a big city like that, coming from a place like this?"

"Do you?" When Vera didn't like the line of questioning she redirected.

"Of course I do. I mean Connecticut is no New York, but I'm still some southern gentleman in a sea of Yankees. You can't find any good soul food. And I miss my family."

"So you'll move back home after you take the bar?" She didn't like how hard it was to figure him out. Was he brilliant? Was he a slacker, faking his way through school with charm and lies?

"I don't plan that far ahead."

"How far ahead do you plan?"

"I like to have at least the next five minutes figured out. I find that's just enough to keep my head above water."

Vera waited for him to start laughing, but he didn't. "You're kidding right? That's not even possible. You don't know what you're doing tomorrow? Next week?"

"I have a rough idea. I'm hoping there are more pancakes at Betty's house. Maybe French toast if I'm lucky. You and I will argue. I'll prove you wrong and get the opportunity to see your nose crinkle up like earlier today. Then I'll go to bed and do it all over again the day after that."

"You can't live that way. No one can."

"How far ahead do you plan your life?"

She reached into her bag and pulled out two books. "Are we talking about day to day? This is my day planner. This is my goals journal. I have a budget in the back and a financial forecast." She flipped through the pages proudly.

"And what happens when you lose those books?" Jay gave a cocky grin. "That would put a crimp in your day."

"I'd be able to access my digital version. These are more or less visual aids." She tucked the books back into her bag. "Having a plan gets you from point A to point B."

"And what happens when things don't go according to plan?"

"I just showed you." She straightened her back confidently. "When things don't go right, you hit something with a rock."

CHAPTER 5

The shop was small and cluttered but welcoming at the same time. Vera hadn't been joking about the huge neon sign. You truly couldn't miss it on the dark winding road.

"I need to find the keys." Vera flipped on the lights in the small office and started looking around. "I come and organize the office and by the next school break it looks like this again. He's hopeless."

"I'm sure he has a system. Like you."

"No." Vera lifted up a huge ring of keys and laughed. "There are a hundred keys on this thing. That is not a system. That's a hot mess."

"So you get your organizational skills from your mother then?" Jay wasn't one to pry. His own privacy was paramount to him and sharing details of his life was something he avoided. But Vera was like this secret location. A mysterious landmark. And finding out how she was formed seemed imperative.

"I wouldn't know. It's always just been my father and me. Apparently, according to my dad, my mother wasn't cut out for motherhood." Vera flipped through the key ring, looking for the one she needed.

"I'm sorry." Jay stepped back and tried to busy himself by looking at all the photos in mismatched frames along the wall.

"Don't be sorry. The only thing I regret is all the time I spent dancing between the idea I did something wrong to make her leave and hoping maybe she'd come back someday. My father and I have done fine on our own. I think it would be worse to have parents who stayed together out of some sense of obligation." She tossed the key ring on the desk in defeat. "There's a few cars out back my dad loans out when people are having repairs done. He keeps the keys in the visors."

"I really appreciate you bailing me out on this. I've basically been a pain in your ass the entire day and plan to be for weeks to come. It's a real testament to your character that you're still willing to help me." He put his hand in his pockets and tried to look as genuine as possible.

"If Betty wants you here, she must have a good reason. I don't know what it is, but I don't really want to go toe to toe with her about not being hospitable to her friend. Plus I can deal with a challenge. You won today, but I'm not in this for a sprint. To me it's a marathon."

He imagined her running toward some finish line as if that was what life was about. "I'm not competing with you, Vera; I think we could work together. Michael picked my case because he saw the potential in it. I was thinking outside the box. But I'm not sure I'll be able to do anything with the case without you."

"Why's that?" She folded her arms and looked at him skeptically.

"Because the inside of my mind looks a hell of a lot like this office. I don't have notebooks or planners. I have ideas, but I'm finding that without proper execution, they don't get me too far. Maybe I've been waiting for someone like you to come help me out."

"I wasn't looking for someone else to help out. My whole life has been scraping to make ends meet, fighting for a voice. I don't feel like I have room to help someone else out. I'm lucky I can keep my own head above water most days." The far off look in her eyes pinched at his chest. Her struggle was real and not far under the surface.

"I'm going to promise you something." He licked his dry lips and took a few steps closer to her. The smell of her perfume was subtle, but he'd been noticing it all day. In this moment he placed it. Gardenias. Sweet and intoxicating, it reminded him of hot summer nights lying on the beach by the dunes.

"Promise me what?"

"At the end of this summer you won't regret I came here. You'll be glad you met me."

Before she could twist her face into a disbelieving or sarcastic expression, there was a moment. She looked hopeful. Impressed even. But it was masked a second later. "Betty would tell you not to write checks you can't cash."

"I promise." He was stone-faced and dangerously close to her now.

"Whatever." She pushed by him and headed for the door. "The only thing worse than treating Betty's friends poorly is making her worry. I'd bet a week's worth of auto parts sales she's out on the porch right now, wondering when you're coming home."

"No one's ever done that for me before," Jay said absentmindedly. It wasn't until he saw her look of concern that he realized he'd revealed more than he wanted to. Either that or she was more astute than the average person, and he was more comfortable than usual.

"Your folks don't worry about you? My dad gets an ulcer every time we go more than day without talking."

"My parents give me a long leash. But it's good. I like the freedom."

Vera led the way to the parking lot where the small two-door car was parked.

"Our apartment is right there. I'm sure my dad is watching from the window right now with lots of questions. Just maybe swing by in the morning and pick me up."

"Sure." Jay took the keys and glanced casually at the two-story apartment where one light was on. "Tell your dad thanks. I'll let Betty know the car is here."

"Night." She waved him off but he waited there, the window down, just looking at her. "What?"

"I'm going to wait until you get to your door over there." He gestured at her apartment and shrugged. "I might not always have a plan, but I always have manners."

She took a few steps toward her apartment and then stopped, turning slightly toward him, her long hair flipping over her shoulder. "Why Mary-Lee Stevens? Why did that case catch your eye?" He could see her brain working overtime. How had he actually won Michael's approval before she could?

He scrambled for an answer that might bring her a little peace. "I had this teacher once; he was funny. Every lesson was a joke. I mean he was quick-witted, but I swear he also wrote material for class. Things I never thought any human could make funny. Heavy stuff no one ever wanted to talk about."

"It wasn't in bad taste?"

"Somehow it wasn't. We all took it for what it was, trying to bring a little levity to something harsh and unforgiving. One day we were discussing the case of a woman who died in prison before she could be exonerated. She'd finally won an appeal, but before the trial date was set she died of lymphoma. He looked at all of us and said: anyone innocent who serves even a day in prison has been wronged. But an innocent mother stuck in prison was the biggest injustice of all. He didn't crack a joke. He didn't follow it with any explanation; I actually think he just walked out. That stuck with me."

"You're sure this is the case we should work on?" She drew in a breath and looked at him expectantly. He'd been filtering all of this through a selfish lens and only now did he see clearly. She needed this to work. Her career was her life raft and right now he was threatening to tip it over. The internship mattered to her. Her reputation mattered because it was her way out. And she wanted out.

"Yesterday I wouldn't have been so sure about any case. I'd have this loop running in my head about all the things I suck at that I'd never be able to pull off. But that was yesterday."

"And today?"

"Today I met you and that voice in my head reminding me what's impossible—it's a hell of a lot quieter."

She dropped her head and gave a little hard-to-read nod. Was she agreeing? Was she grateful? Annoyed? It was one more bit of confusion and mystery to add to what she already was to him.

"Night, Jay." She sighed as she moved toward her front door. Damn, he liked hearing her say his name.

CHAPTER 6

She should have asked him for the records. Vera berated herself for being so distracted. If she had the details of the case file, she could have stayed up that night and gotten ahead of the game. Maybe she could have even knocked enough holes in his theory to get Michael to change his mind and pick one of her cases instead.

Competitiveness was a curse and a blessing. In this situation she wasn't sure which it would turn out to be. Jay seemed like an all right guy. He certainly had charm, and that stupid kind of smile that took over his whole face. His eyes would squint and his cheeks would rise. That had been what kept her from being at the top of her game. But it would be different today.

Her father was already dressed in his blue mechanic coveralls as he poured himself a cup of coffee. His wispy combed-over hair was sticking up and his eyes were sleepy.

"So this stranger who stole one of my cars last night, do I need to hunt him down?"

"I told you last night, he's staying with Betty and working with Michael. Betty lent him her car and the starter died last night." She didn't make eye contact with her dad because he knew her too well. He'd start asking questions she wouldn't want to answer.

"Two interns?"

"Yeah, trust me, I'm not crazy about it. Jay's aunt grew up with Betty, and she's doing her a favor. But it'll put a damper on my summer."

He leaned against the kitchen counter and got that look. The one that always pierced Vera's heart. His round face would sink a little and his thick overgrown brows would wrinkle together. "I know you wanted to intern in the city this year. It would have really helped your career."

"Dad, it's fine. Being home this summer and working at the shop, staying home for free, that's how I'll afford staying in the city next summer. I'll be one year closer to taking the bar. And I'm sure if I do well with Michael, any connections he has to firms in New York will be pleased."

He sighed and sipped his steaming hot coffee. "I wish this was all easier for you. I wish I would've put money away for college."

"What money?" She laughed. "We spent what we had on things we needed. That's all. I'm telling you, Dad, this is fine. I'm going to learn a lot this summer. It might not be as much networking as I would've had in the city, but I'm going to have autonomy. Michael's trust in me is what makes the difference. I can really do some good here."

"Does he have you working on something?" Her father perked up and the lump growing in the back of her throat dissolved. She only wanted him to be proud, not bogged down with regret and worry.

"Yeah, there's not enough work to do for the two of us, so he's letting Jay and me spend some time and resources on a case. There's a woman in South Carolina who went to prison decades ago for poisoning her baby. We're going to see if we can dig into that."

"She didn't do it?" His eyes opened wide and his simple sweet optimism made her smile.

"I don't know, Dad. We're going to be looking more at the prosecution to make sure she got a fair trial."

"Hmm," he hummed, looking less enthusiastic now. "The law is a tricky thing. Bad people walk free, good people get locked up. It's scary."

"I didn't pick the case. I keep thinking the same thing. What if she did do this, and we're the ones who get her out? That's a pretty terrible thing."

"You'll know what's right, and you'll do what's right." He'd been saying that for years. So often that it rang in her head in the quiet moments of her life that required a choice. But she had made mistakes. She'd hurt people to get ahead, and she wasn't proud of that. Now when her father said this she only felt guilt. He still believed she was the little girl in the pigtails, defending the kids on the playground from the bullies. He'd never believe she'd been a bully herself while away at college.

"I don't always do what's right, Dad." She gulped as she slipped her shoes on. "I screw up."

"I don't want you to be perfect, Vera. You're supposed to make some mistakes. That way, when the big questions come, when you really have to decide something that matters, you'll remember what it feels like to make the mistake, and you'll choose the right path. It's like when you were learning to ride your bike and I took one training wheel off. It was just enough to give you a sense of what you needed to do when the other one came off."

"You give me too much credit." She peered out the kitchen window and saw Jay pulling up to the front of the apartment building. "I've got to go." She rushed by and planted a kiss on his cheek.

"The boy is picking you up in one of my cars?" He put his mug down and followed her out to the front steps.

"Morning, sir," Jay called as he put the car in park and stepped out. She wanted to whack him. This was meant to be a drive-by where he barely slowed down, and she jumped in. Her father always got weird around guys her age. "I really appreciate you lending me the car last night."

"I didn't." He puffed up his chest and glared at Jay.

"Well um, I appreciate that you raised a daughter who was kind enough to lend me a car last night. I'll cover the cost of any repairs to Betty's car. I spoke with her this morning, and she said she'd give you a call."

As her father leaned over the rail of the front steps, Vera knew it was coming. A pit of dread planted in her stomach. "My daughter isn't like other girls. She's not charmed by the stories boys like you tell. She won't cave to whatever pressures you're considering. She's got her own mind."

To Jay's credit he didn't flinch or show a look of shock. Instead he moved toward the porch and shook the man's calloused and grease stained hands. "She's already put me in my place about a dozen times, and we only met yesterday. You've raised a good one."

"Damn right." The handshake broke, and Jay waited to be dismissed. "Drive like a normal person, don't go revving the engine to try to show off."

"Bye, Dad," Vera groaned but punctuated it with a smile.

"He's like a real dad, huh?" Jay asked as he backed slowly out of the driveway.

"You got off easy. If you wouldn't have known to get out of that car and shake his hand you would have really been in for it." She reached back to his bag and opened it.

"Can I help you?"

"I want to read the files." She pulled them out and opened the papers onto her lap.

"We're going to be at Michael's office in a few minutes. You can read them then."

Her finger was flying over the notes as she turned the pages quickly. "I should have grabbed a copy last night. I'm behind now."

"Behind what?"

"Behind you. You're way more familiar with the case than I am, and once we finish all the busy work in the office Michael is going to ask for an update. I'd like to be able to give him one."

"We can work on it together once we get through the other stuff. I don't think Michael is pitting us against each other in some attempt to thin the herd. It's not a competition."

"Anyone who says that is always trying to win. Life is a competition. There is no logical way I should be in law school right now. Single parent home. Living at the poverty line. I didn't go to private school. I didn't have a single connection. But when there was something to be done, I made sure I did it first and did it best. That's my edge. I'm not going to lose just because you are all —" She stopped abruptly and choked on her words.

"I'm all what?" he pressed. "Handsome? Charming? Disarmingly funny?"

"Flaky," she corrected. "Unmotivated. Indifferent. I'm not letting that rub off on me."

"I'm pretty sure your father won't allow anything of mine to rub off on you."

"Don't be stupid," she scolded. "You know what I mean. You might not take this seriously, but I'm going to. Yesterday I was overconfident. I tried to pick cases I thought would be easy to overturn, but I should have known Michael wouldn't be driven by that metric. He's affected by humanity and all its different layers. You tapped into that and you won."

"Again," he said with a laugh, "not a contest. We're learning. We're trying to do something noble that represents the best part of our legal system. Checks and balances. The right to a fair trial. You're making it sound like we're in a relay race and I'm cheating at the potato sack part."

"How can you cheat at the potato sack race?" she asked, twisting up her face. "You get in a sack and you jump. You know, if you're going to use analogies in the courtroom someday, you're going to need to give them more thought."

"Thanks for the advice." He pulled the car into a parking spot and sat for a moment. "I'm being serious, Vera. I don't want to be your competition. I want to do this together."

"Why?"

"Two reasons. One: if this is a competition of any kind, I'll lose to you. Unless it becomes some kind of eating contest because I have won ribbons for that."

"And what's the other reason?"

"You're in law school. You know what it's like. Every person for themselves. Everything is about solidifying the future and being better than the person sitting next to you. This is summer. When I was a kid, it was what I looked forward to all year long. Laughing. Playing. Taking chances. We don't have a lot of opportunities to do that at school. Maybe we can make this summer something better."

"That's hokey." She clutched the files to her chest, staking claim. "And it sounds like something you would say to trick me into having fun."

"You need to be tricked into having fun?"

She didn't answer as they got out of the car and headed into the office. She knew this would never get old. Walking into a place, even one as small as this one, where law was being practiced, gave her chills. She'd known what she wanted to be since she was ten years old. There was something finite about the law. Someone else crafted it. Someone else enforced it. Her job would be to apply it. It couldn't get more predetermined than that. It was red plus blue becoming purple. It just was. And that was something she could live with.

CHAPTER 7

"We need to change this while we still have time." Vera's voice was high and urgent. "I think we could just piggyback on a case that one of the more experienced justice projects has worked. We're two college kids working within the confines of a very small firm and this case is way out of our league."

"If this was an old movie someone would come along and slap you in the face to snap you out of this." He didn't want to mock her, but he couldn't fight the smile. "How do you get through finals with this wound-up energy?"

"This isn't a final, Jay. It's not textbooks and essays. This is real life. They just emailed over the rest of the court documents. It's over a thousand pages. We'll spend our entire summer trying to get our arms around the details. I need something concrete this year. I need a win."

"Vera, I've got this. I might not have your GPA or your book smarts. Anyone can tell from a mile away that you are smarter than I am. But I don't get bogged down in the minutiae. I'll look at this case and dissect what the weak points were and we'll start there. I say the first thing we do is lay out a timeline. How did the crime happen according to testimony? Then we look for character witnesses that didn't testify to try to understand what was happening with Mary-Lee at the time."

"Yeah." She nodded her head and looked like she was coming down from her panic. "I guess we can start there."

He grabbed a marker and took to the white board. "We know Mary-Lee had one child six years prior. When she divorced her husband, the child, whose name is redacted from the court records, went to live with his father."

"That right there is a red flag." Vera made a note in her book. "She previously abandoned a child."

"We don't know the circumstances of her divorce. She didn't lose custody, nor were there any allegations of abuse or neglect. Children do live with one parent when the parents divorce."

"Look here," she slid a paper over to him. "After her second son, Pauly, was born, her doctor noted signs of postpartum depression."

"You're jumping ahead. Mary-Lee marries again, a man named Daryl Stevens, and a year later they had baby Pauly. Prenatal reports were all normal and her labor and delivery had nothing out of the ordinary."

"The doctor testified he had thirteen trips to his pediatrician in addition to normal well visits, according to the notes he put on their file. They mentioned she seemed nervous and abnormally concerned about Pauly's health."

"Abnormally?"

Jay shrugged. "That's a generalization. Parents all react differently to parenthood."

Vera tilted her head and looked at him with disbelief. "She was referred to a psychiatrist to deal with postpartum depression five months before Pauly died. The doctor testified he did believe she was suffering from exhaustion and PPD."

Jay wasn't budging off his side of the argument. "But she never discussed thoughts of hurting Pauly or hurting herself.

She's one of millions of women who get the diagnosis and don't go on to hurt their children."

"I'm taking the stance of a jury member," Vera explained. "This is how they would react to this information. We have to keep that in mind. If there ever is a retrial, she'll face these same issues."

"That was part of the problem in the first trial. There were eleven women and one man. All were either parents or grandparents. Jury selection was weak." Jay smiled. One point for him.

"You know as well as I do that's not grounds for an appeal." She leaned back in her chair as he filled in more of the timeline.

"The week of Pauly's death, Mary-Lee's husband was away on a business trip in Utah. He came home and reported that Pauly seemed all right. That night Pauly was sick. He'd had a few stomach bugs over the months prior and when he vomited Daryl thought he was starting with another one. When the vomiting continued and Pauly seemed lethargic and hard to wake, they got nervous and took him to the emergency room."

"Right." Vera stood and grabbed a marker. He knew she couldn't help herself. "Then the report says the emergency room doctors grew concerned by Mary-Lee's behavior. She was detached and aloof. Not concerned enough about the baby's well-being. They conducted blood work and found high levels of ethylene glycol. There's a lot of medical jargon here we'd need to dig into. His symptoms and such. They put Pauly in protective custody and the police were called. The ER doctor testified that he believed Mary-Lee had been poisoning Pauly with antifreeze."

"The police searched the home and found a bottle of antifreeze in the garage." Jay shook his head. "Just like most garages in America."

"Did they test any of the bottles or bowls the baby used to eat?" Vera flipped through the documents in her hand. "I don't see that they did."

"No. They took the antifreeze into evidence but nothing else. At this point Pauly was alive and seeming to respond well to the hospital stay. For three days he was kept away from Mary-Lee and Daryl, and he seemed to improve."

Vera practically shoved him aside. "They made their case to the police. She was distraught and wanted to be with her sick child. They made arrangements for her to have a few brief visits with Pauly. Two days after Mary-Lee's last visit he took a turn for the worse and died."

"They pulled Daryl and Mary-Lee into the police station and began interrogating them. Daryl had a solid alibi according to the police since he was out of town leading up the Pauly's initial hospital visit. He also never visited Pauly once he was put in protective custody. It had been two weeks since he'd had any contact. The police ruled him out as a suspect, which left only Mary-Lee."

"There isn't much here about what Daryl had to say about the situation. He never testified in court, but the officers who took the stand referenced some of his statements in the initial interrogation. He didn't dismiss the idea that his wife might have killed Pauly," Vera said.

"You're pushing it there," Jay challenged, pointing his marker at her. "Officers led Daryl to believe she had failed a lie detector test, which was not true. She never took one. The line of questioning by the police was very inflammatory, and he'd just lost his only son. He was distraught. After her arrest he borrowed money and mortgaged their house to pay for an attorney for her. Once cooler heads prevailed and the shock wore off, news reports implied he was in her corner."

"But he didn't testify on her behalf?"

"You know that no sane defense attorney would put him up there. It's emotional and a liability to the case."

"Because he might tell the truth. He might tell everyone his wife was sad and upset, and if he was under oath he might be compelled to admit he, for at least a short period of time, considered she did it."

Michael popped his head in. "You two need to eat. Betty already warned me if I let you work through lunch she'll find out. Jules is bringing by some sandwiches. Make sure you eat them."

"Have you met her?" Vera asked Jay as the sound of Michael's shoes moved farther away.

"Who, his wife, Jules? No not yet. That's Betty's daughter?"

"Yeah, she's the best. When I was growing up, she was really nice to me. I didn't know a thing about putting on lipstick or anything like that. Jules always saw me at their family restaurant and would give me little pointers about things. Someday when I'm a lawyer and I get my life together, I'm going to get her something. I don't know what, but something special."

It was glimpse, a flash of the humanity Vera tried hard to camouflage behind tough talk and staying insanely busy. "I'm sure she'd appreciate that."

"I guess I shouldn't jinx it. It's a matter of if. I have a long way to go before I consider myself a success." She bit at her lip and flipped absentmindedly through some papers in the large stack of files. "I think that's the hardest part of all of this. I've been telling people for so long exactly how my life is going to turn out, and now they expect it. Some are even depending on it."

"Nothing is set in stone. You can always change your mind about things."

"If anyone around here heard you say that, they'd know we'd just met. My mind is like stone."

A cheerful voice cut in as a red-headed woman in a pink sundress pranced into the room. "Stone is changed all the time." She beamed with a playful smile. "Just ask a river. Nothing cuts a rock down like a river."

"You must be Jules," Jay said, sticking his hand out for a shake.

"We hug here, son." Jules pulled him in and squeezed him tightly.

"She's not hugging you," Michael interrupted. "She's seeing if you're all skin and bones so she can force you to have two sandwiches."

"The boy works out," Jules reported, sounding disappointed. "But he's having pie."

"No argument from me on that," Jay answered, eyeing the basket on her arm.

Jules took over the small piece of real estate on the conference room table that wasn't taken up by the case file mess.

"Michael tells me you two are taking on quite the task." She glanced up at the white board and winced. They hadn't been particularly polished in their notes. Some of it was downright cold. Jules winced as she read them. "You sure picked a doozy of a case. I can't imagine."

Jay felt the need to explain. "I know the idea of a mother hurting her child is not easy to think about. It's the kind of crime that can't be sorted out easily in most people's minds."

"I know that," Jules said, with a curious look. "I mean I can't imagine losing your child then getting put in a cage to think about it for the rest of your life. If she didn't do it, I can't think of a worse existence."

Jay froze. He hadn't expected that reaction. After a long awkward moment he finally edged out a reply. "Yeah, that's true."

"Do you think she did it?" Jules asked as she handed out sandwiches and cans of soda.

Vera chimed in first. "It's too soon to tell. The evidence suggests she had motive and opportunity. She was being treated for postpartum depression. I think she was tired."

Jules laughed then stifled it. "Sorry, it's not funny. The word tired doesn't begin to capture the feeling you have with a baby around. It's this out-of-body, bone-deep exhaustion that convinces you you'll never feel rested again. I was treated for postpartum depression after Frankie was born. She needed so much, and I kept thinking I should be happy. Why am I not happy when I have everything? But your mind can play tricks on you when you're tired and hungry and scared."

"I didn't know that." Vera looked sheepish as she took in the news. "You're so tough. I've seen you do some crazy mama bear stuff over the years."

"I had a good support system," Jules reported. "I bounced back quickly. I'm not saying I think anyone should hurt their child. I'm only saying I can see the very dark and twisting path that leads to that. I hate that it exists, but I know it does."

Jay unwrapped the brown paper from the masterpiece of a sandwich. "Thanks for lunch. We wouldn't have eaten if you hadn't brought it."

"I figured. If you two need anything else, let me know. I'm always good for a meal and some unsolicited advice."

"Have any for us now?" Vera asked with a sweet smile.

"I can only give you some from my perspective as a mother and as the wife of a lawyer. Don't underestimate the power a case can have on you. You can try to stay disconnected from it, try not to let it get personal, but it will. The second you two get past the white board stage and actually dig into the real people involved it will get real very quickly. It'll stir things you may never have considered before. We all have baggage, and nothing pulls it out from the dark corners we tuck it into like the journey you two are about to take."

"You know me," Vera laughed. "I don't get emotionally tied up in junk. It's all about logistics and getting answers."

"Oh I know, sweetheart." Jules sighed. "You're tough as nails. Logical. Fierce. I love that about you. I think that's why I'm giving you the warning. You're going to have a moment; you're going to look into someone's eyes along the way and realize these aren't names on a court document. Make sure when that happens you have someone with you who gets it." Jules looked over at Jay in a knowing way. And he gave a tiny nod.

He got it. Vera saw the world as a set of circumstances. A checklist. A race to run with a finish line. There was a good chance this experience might challenge that reality for her. He knew better than most what shattering information you've always known to be accurate could do to a person.

"Oh please," Vera laughed. "I love this stuff. This is a task. It's a challenge. You know I love challenges."

"You do." Jules gave a sweet smile and opened one of the files near her as she took a bite of her sandwich. It was a snapshot of Pauly, one of those pictures people used to go into the mall studio and get. He was propped up on a fuzzy brown carpet wearing blue overalls and a white collared shirt. His smile was wide, and his chin glistening with drool. "Sweet angel," Jules whispered. "I hope you get answers."

"We will," Jay said adamantly, drawing everyone's eyes to him. "I can tell Vera and I are going to make one hell of a team."

Michael wheeled his chair closer to Jules and put his arm around her. "Don't they remind you of Piper and Bobby when they first met?"

"Yeah, they do."

Jay didn't know who that was and didn't bother asking. He could infer that his dynamic with Vera would be a spirited one. Push and pull. And whoever Piper and Bobby were, he hoped they'd survived their early days and were not some cautionary tale Jules gave as a warning.

Edenville was this strange little town, a village really, and if he had a chance to be in the cast of characters, he wouldn't pass it up.

Michael finished his lunch and tossed the trash in the bin across the room like an NBA player. "I'm all for you two cracking this case and getting your names on the news, but I still need copies of the legal briefs I asked for. Don't forget you're my interns first and private detectives second."

Vera hopped up and tossed her lunch too. "I'll have them ready in ten minutes."

Michael fixed his eyes on Jay with a challenging grin. "Why don't you jump up like that? Give her some competition."

"I would," Jay began, watching Vera with affection. "But it's like I'd run the Kentucky Derby by foot compared to her. I don't stand a chance."

Jules rose and kissed her husband on his cheek. "He's a smart boy."

CHAPTER 8

"I don't think we know enough to know if the prosecution did anything wrong." The lights in the conference room were humming. The rest of the office building was dark. Everyone else had gone home. But the hours felt like minutes when you were ticking things off a to-do list. It was Vera's favorite feeling.

"We're law students. We should."

"I'm a first-year law student, and you're one who is flunking out of school. If this were easier more people would do it. All I'm saying is we might be able to ask for an appeal based on improper representation or misconduct by the prosecution, but we don't even know what we're looking for."

"I don't think we should start there. I think we should follow the avenue of finding new evidence," Jay responded.

"You know how hard that is?" Vera took another sip of her iced coffee and let the caffeine jolt her mind. "Especially in a case like this. There's no real weapon. I doubt the crime scene or evidence was preserved all these years."

"We need to talk to people. We need to start interviewing people who knew them at the time. I don't see much in the police report about that. They arrested Mary-Lee and they let the doctors decide she had to be the one who had done it."

"Based on science." Vera was still feeling like this was a bad choice. The case was messy. She hated messy. Questions should have answers.

"Science from decades ago. We used to stick leaches on people to cure them of diseases. The world evolves. I'm telling you, the best thing we can do is get a sense from other people of what kind of mother Mary-Lee was."

"And we just pick up the phone and start calling people?"

"Yes. Why not?"

"I guess my question is, who the hell are we?" Vera's confident approach to everything seemed to be cracking.

"We are two associates with this law firm, calling on behalf of Michael Cooper. We've taken an interest in the case and want to follow up."

"Hell no." Vera folded her arms across her chest. "We don't have any idea what we're doing. Michael isn't going to want us dropping his name and acting like we're more than we are."

"Oh please." Jay waved her off.

"What?"

"Vera, you could take the bar tomorrow if you wanted and pass. I don't think acting like you are more than you are is the problem."

"Oh no, then what's the problem?"

"You're scared, and you're biased as hell. You see this woman who abandoned one child and might have hurt the second and you see your own situation. You don't want to help her. In your future job, you won't be able to factor in your emotions. There's no room for it."

"Go to hell," Vera shouted, her blood instantly boiling. "You don't know a damn thing about me." She pulled out the keys and tossed them to him. "Lock up the office when you're done playing detective and fooling yourself into believing this is going to work out."

"Where are you going?"

"Home."

"I'm your ride." Jay shot to his feet and raced after her.

"I can walk." She put her hair over her shoulder and pushed her way out the door. The summer night air was thick, but she didn't care. There was no way she was getting in the car with him.

"It's two miles. You aren't walking home alone in the dark."

"Watch me. As a matter of fact, don't. This isn't going to work out. I'm done. You do whatever you want with this woman and this case, and I'm going to do the office work I expected to when I got the internship. Just leave me out of it." She headed in the direction of her house and ignored his apologies. He was downright begging her now to get in the car as he hopped in and the engine roared to life.

"Just go."

"I can't let you walk home. Please, Betty will find out. She'll kill me. I already messed up her car. I don't want to piss her off. She'll stop making me breakfast."

"This isn't a game to me, Jay. I'm not trying to get a rise out of you. I'm very serious right now. I'm done. I take calculated risks. I would work on a case that we actually had odds of making progress on. I don't waste time. I don't start something I know will fail."

"Is walking home alone a calculated risk?"

"If I'm comparing it to getting in the car, killing you, and serving life in prison, yes. I'm playing the right odds."

"Fine, I'm following you then." He put the car in drive and crept slowly behind her as she walked to her house. "You're being ridiculous."

"You are driving two miles an hour down the road. Which one of us is ridiculous?"

"There are like coyotes and stuff out here."

A car pulled up behind them and blue and red lights burst to life. A cop. Vera felt a knot in her stomach. Everyone in town would now know about this drama tomorrow now.

"Pull over," a voice over the car's loudspeaker called. Jay reluctantly moved the car off the road and made a move to get out. Bad decision.

Bobby put his hand on his gun and shouted. "Get back in the vehicle and keep your hands where I can see them. Vera, you okay?"

Jay obeyed but drowned her answer out with his own explanation. "I told her not to walk home, it's not safe. I was following her."

"You were following her?" Bobby asked angrily as he closed in on the car, his hand still at the ready. "And she didn't want you to?"

"No, she didn't."

"Then you and I have a problem." Bobby swung the car door open and yanked Jay out. He pressed him against the car and put cuffs on him. "Vera, hop in my car. Your dad was looking for you. I'll call him and tell him you're all right."

"My cell phone died," she explained, realizing how late it was and how worried her dad must be.

"Why are you cuffing me?" Jay asked through a grunt as Bobby spun him around and patted him down.

"Attempted kidnapping, stalking. I don't know yet."

"Vera, could you tell him I wasn't trying to kidnap you?" Jay pleaded. There was a brief moment where she considered letting him spend a night in a holding cell just to get some points against him. But she didn't have it in her.

"He's Michael's other intern. He's staying with Betty." Vera's explanation was reluctant. "He wasn't technically trying to kidnap me."

Bobby stopped patting him down but didn't make a move to take the cuffs off. "So why was he following you slowly in the car?"

"Because he pissed me off, and I wanted to walk home."

"What did you do to piss her off?" Bobby's grip was tight, and he spoke through gritted teeth. "Did you try something with her? Because Betty will have your bags in the street if you did."

"I told her she was afraid to take on the case we're working on. Apparently she doesn't like being called afraid." Jay looked at her with a mix of need and apology. "I was trying to figure her out. That was a big mistake."

"Am I taking the cuffs off him, Vera?" Bobby waited, looking between the two of them for an answer.

"Yeah, he's harmless. Annoying but harmless." She shrugged and started walking toward her apartment.

"You aren't going to let her walk home are you?" Jay asked with an edge of worry in his voice.

"Oh hell kid, you've got it bad for her already?" He chuckled and took the cuffs off. "Vera, my car or his, but you're taking a ride from someone. If I let you walk home, your dad will hang me by my toes from the car lift."

Bobby's radio burst to life with static and then voices. He was getting another call from dispatch. "If you come with me we're stopping to deal with a stranded motorist."

"Fine," Vera huffed. "I'll ride with Jay, but can you tell him not to talk to me?"

Bobby grabbed Jay's arm before he could get back in the driver's seat. "If you talk to her I will find you. I will slap these cuffs back on and drop you in the woods at the foot of the mountains. Then I'll hunt you. I won't kill you, I can't do that, but I will make sure when you come out of the woods you'll never be the same."

Vera grinned as Jay gulped and nodded.

"Vera, don't make your dad worry. Keep your phone charged, tell him where you'll be. And no matter how annoying someone is, don't walk home. You can always call one of us. You know we'd come get you no matter what. You're like one of our own."

"I know." She sucked her lip in and dropped her head down. For all the time she spent wondering why she wasn't enough to keep her mom around, these people reminded her she could be loved. "Sorry."

"And you." Bobby grabbed Jay again. "You don't know what you're messing with when you mess with her. Tread lightly."

"Michael and Jules said she and I remind them a lot of you and Piper. Is that a good thing?"

Bobby laughed as he tucked his handcuffs back on his belt. "Sure, it's great. If you like chaos, constant bickering, and interjecting yourselves pretty regularly into dangerous situations."

CHAPTER 9

"Child." Betty stood on the porch with her foot tapping and her arms crossed. "I'm going to set you a curfew."

"Sorry, Betty." Jay slinked his way up the steps and sat with a sigh on the porch swing. "It was a rough night."

"Bobby already called me." Betty took a seat in her rocking chair. "You were lucky Vera let you off the hook."

"She almost didn't." He rubbed his wrists where the handcuffs had been. "I'm not here trying to cause problems."

"But are you here for something?"

"An internship." His simple answer didn't seem to convince her. "And I'm grateful for you arranging it. I'm just not sure Vera and I can work together. She hates me."

Betty let out a little sigh and rocked her squeaky chair. "Yeah, I'm sure she does."

"Thanks?"

"Vera hates new things. She hates surprising things. You're both. She keeps her circle small and her plan tight. It's what keeps her safe."

"From what?" The hair on his arms stood up as he imagined

Vera in any kind of danger. He already felt the pull to protect her, though she hardly seemed like she needed it.

"You're a smart kid, you'll figure it out. But that's the easy part. The hard part is what to do once you know. Knowing doesn't change anything."

"Is this a haiku?" Jay smirked and leaned back on the porch swing. The night was quiet and the yard danced with fireflies.

"Of the two of us, I don't think I'm the mystery here." Moths fluttered up to the light above Betty's head. The light cast a halo, which, judging by the words of everyone who knew her, was fitting.

"I'm no mystery. Just a guy with crappy grades and a track record of failing in general. I think that's what pisses Vera off so much. I'm some slacker idiot, screwing with her opportunity."

"So then, maybe, go home?" Betty reached into a basket near her chair and pulled out knitting needles and a half-finished baby blanket.

"I can't." The words flew out before he realized he might need to explain them.

"Didn't think so."

The porch swing squeaked as Jay got up. If he stayed much longer she'd get every last secret out of him. She was obviously that good.

"I'm going to turn in. You need anything?"

She gave him a long scrutinizing look. "I can read people like a book. I know pain. I know defiance. I know evil. All usually at first glance. Maybe I'm getting old. Maybe I'm losing my special powers, but I'll be damned, you I'm not sure about."

Jay paused, thinking before sighing and giving in to Betty's . . . whatever this was. "When I was little I had this magic set. The tricks were easy, but I learned the key to all of it was misdirection. Hiding in plain sight. I guess I got good at doing that."

"But you're one of the good ones still?"

"I try to be."

"Then I'll save my scary warning about the consequences of crossing someone I care about."

"Don't worry." Jay chuckled. "Bobby did a damn good job of that already tonight."

CHAPTER 10

Betty must have given him those damn flowers from her garden. "I have allergies," Vera said as she leaned away from the bouquet.

"Then I'll put them in a vase way over here and you can just look at them." Jay filled the small glass pitcher with water and put the flowers on the windowsill. "I just wanted to say I was sorry about yesterday. You know how it is, you take a few psych courses in college and all of a sudden you feel like you've got everyone around you figured out. I don't know what I was talking about."

"Yeah." Vera shrugged and busied herself with the papers on the conference room table. "I was up last night and I think I figured something out."

"What?" He dusted the pollen off his hands and took the seat next to her. He was anxious, a spark of enthusiasm he'd been holding back.

"You were right about the witness testimony. It was all doctors, and most of what they said had little to do with science and more to do with speculation. There were almost no cold hard facts being discussed. The most interesting witness to me was Dr.

Edward Fraylink. He was the ER doctor who admitted Pauly and first suspected the parents of wrongdoing."

"What do you know about him?"

"He'd only been working there for a month. He was as inexperienced in his job as you and I are right now. The case hinged on his testimony, and he'd hardly been a doctor for a month. He's the person who read the results of the blood test. It's probably the first time he'd ever encountered that reading of glycol in the blood."

"Good." Jay took her notes and scanned them. She hated her physical need for approval. In school it always drove her nuts to not only be teacher's pet, but to desperately want to be. It was just who she was. "I think we should talk to the husband, Pauly's father."

"I read a little bit about him last night. He's remarried, has three children, and doesn't seem to discuss the case at all anymore. No interviews. No nothing."

Jay started typing something into his computer and a minute later he was hitting the speakerphone on the landline and grinning.

"What are you doing?" Vera's heart was thudding. He couldn't actually be calling Daryl Stevens.

"We're going to talk to him."

"This is not how you conduct a follow up interview—"

"Hello?"

"Ah hi, yes is this Daryl Stevens?"

"It is, who's speaking?"

"My name is Jay Crowly. I was hoping you had a few minutes to speak with me today."

"In regards to what?" His tone was guarded but he hadn't hung up. Vera on the other hand was seriously contemplating disconnecting the line.

"I'm here with my associate, Vera Pedro. We're reinvestigating Mary-Lee's case, and we wanted to know if you'd be willing to speak with us about it."

The line was silent long enough to make Vera sure he'd hung up. But he cleared throat and went on. "To what end?"

"Excuse me?"

"What are you investigating?"

"The death of Pauly Stevens. We're going to make inquiries and our law firm here in North Carolina may be able to come up with grounds for an appeal. How do you feel about that?"

"How do I feel about that?" Daryl lost his breath for a moment. "I feel like I've been wondering where this call has been for the last couple of decades. It's about time someone tries to help Mary-Lee out."

"So you're willing to talk with us today?" Jay gave Vera a thumbs-up, but she was too angry to get excited. He'd spontaneously called one of the most important witnesses in this case, and they had no plan.

"Yes."

"That's great. I hope you don't mind, for this first discussion we plan to keep it very conversational. It's still early in our investigation, and we're trying to speak to as many people as possible. Do you mind if I record our conversation?"

"No, it's fine."

Jay set up his phone to record. "Thank you. We really appreciate your time this morning. I'm going to jump right in if that's not too jarring. Do you believe Mary-Lee killed your son Pauly?"

"I do. I think she poisoned Pauly."

Jay dropped his head down, looking defeated. This was why you prep. Before he could open his mouth with another question Daryl was explaining.

"I don't think she should be in prison. I never thought she should be."

Vera leaned in toward the phone. "You think she killed your

son but shouldn't have gone to prison?"

"It was my fault."

The hair on the back of Vera's neck stood up. Thank goodness they were tape recording if they were about to get a confession.

"What do you mean?" she pressed.

"I traveled for work. But sometimes I didn't have to go. I was so tired and I needed a minute to relax and be in a quiet space. So I'd schedule a trip out to an office in another part of the country and work there. I knew how much she was struggling, and I was still so damn selfish. I left her right in the thick of it all."

"And you think under the pressure she snapped and poisoned Pauly?" Jay still hadn't regained his voice so Vera kept pressing on. "Is that why you didn't testify on her behalf?"

"I knew under oath I'd do more damage than good. I loved Mary-Lee, and I loved Pauly. You have to understand I lost my entire family that year. I was in shock."

"I understand," Jay said, finally jumping back in. "What made you so sure she was to blame for his death?"

"Well" —Daryl had to think on it for a moment— "the police said the science was solid. There was blood work. We had antifreeze in the house. Then the fact that he died just a day after they finally let her visit in the hospital. I stopped being able to rationalize any other scenario. It was happening more and more on the news. These stories of moms who couldn't cope and did the unthinkable."

"Initially what other scenarios did you consider?" Jay's pen hovered over the notepad as Daryl began to explain.

"I thought maybe someone had broken into the house and poisoned him. Maybe there was someone in Mary-Lee's life I didn't know about. A lover? What if Mary had done it in her sleep? Somehow mixing up the formula with the antifreeze? She was so tired. But everything I came up with led back to her." His voice cracked with emotion.

Vera didn't want to lose him on this call. It could be enough to convince Michael they were wasting time and resources. "Can you tell me about her other son? You said she was a loving mother and devoted. Why did she abandon her first child?"

"Oh I don't think that's exactly how it happened. I never met him, but I know that Mary-Lee was sixteen when she had him. Her first husband was twenty. They had Jeremy and got married. It was a lot but they lasted a while. She never had a bad thing to say about her first husband, but it just fell apart. The guy got a job somewhere else and had more stability in his life. He'd already gotten engaged to someone else, and it seemed to make more sense for Jeremy to live with him. Mary-Lee visited there. I think it was amicable all around. But I knew it was hard for Mary-Lee. There were tears at times. She didn't abandon him, if anything she sacrificed so he could have a good life."

Jay scratched notes down quickly. "So you remarried? Do you have any contact with Mary-Lee?"

"No."

"Why is that?"

"I suppose it's because I can hardly get through Pauly's birthday every year without wanting to drive my car off a bridge. I have a wife and three kids. I couldn't keep one foot in that world and one foot in this one. Mary-Lee sent me a letter after her second appeal failed. She told me to move on. I was taken off her approved visitor list, and she wouldn't take my calls. She completely cut me out. It's a theme in her life, making these huge painful sacrifices for the good of other people even if it rips her up inside. I can't imagine how alone she must feel, but she knew the only way I'd make it was if she forced me to."

Vera cleared her throat and licked at her dry lips. "I'm honestly shocked that you could be so forgiving of a woman you're sure killed your child. It seems counterintuitive."

"I suppose it is but that doesn't change anything. I carry the burden of knowing I left my wife when she probably needed me most. When my kids were born, my three now, I stayed home. I changed diapers. Midnight feedings. I made sure my wife knew I had her back. I believe if I'd have done that for Mary-Lee, Pauly would be alive. That makes it pretty hard to blame and hate her. I'd have to spend all my time feeling the same way about myself."

Jay leaned back in his chair and put his hands on his head, running them through his hair. He looked suddenly exhausted or spent emotionally. Like he was battling something just under the surface. "Is there anything else you'd like to add?"

"I want Mary-Lee to feel the sun on her face again. I want her to be able to put her feet in the ocean. Pauly would want that too. I believe it. So if you are able to help her, please do."

They expressed their gratitude and disconnected the call. Vera had a pretty good sense about situations. She'd treated the skill like a science, measuring little signals. Right now she could feel every little pulse of unease and she wanted answers.

"Jay," Vera began, forcing herself to not look smug, "we have the husband saying he thinks she did it. He was the closest person in her life at the time. If we did help her to get another trial, and he was compelled now to testify, that would be it. As sympathetic and forgiving as he is, he believes she did it. That means even a fairly selected jury would probably too."

"Since when does a witness's opinion decide the case? He didn't see her do anything." Jay stood up and paced the room. There was a desperation that didn't feel rooted to being wrong. She on the other hand would hang on to winning with the death grip, fighting until the end to show she was right. That didn't seem like Jay's style.

It was time to push. That moment in a trial where the attorney bursts with emotion to drive the witness to spill the beans. "You know what, more than that, what the hell are you doing cold calling a witness in a case and pretending to be some kind of legal investigator? You can't throw around Michael's name like that. If we are ever going to do an interview like that again, we're going to have our act together. You don't just dial the phone. That's not how a team works. You're being reckless, and I want to know why. What else is going on here?"

The second the question hit the atmosphere she realized she might not want the answer. There was a risk that it would change something. Slice through the small threads that were now lacing them together. For once the truth felt risky, and maybe a lie wouldn't be so bad if it prolonged their time in these moments.

"Sometimes you do, Vera. That's the point. Sometimes you can think things to death and end up with a great plan but nothing to show for it. You would have hit him with a structured line of questioning, and he'd have been in a defensive posture the whole time. I just wanted to talk to him. I wanted to hear what he had to say, unfiltered."

She could press more. Why did he look so upset? What did this mean to him? But for once the tiger inside of her felt like a new born kitten.

"We're dropping this." Vera stood and gulped hard. "I'm sorry, Jay. I'm telling Michael what happened today. I'll let him hear the recording. He won't let us keep going. He's a good man with a very high standard of ethics, and you were misleading to a victim. We should have gotten Michael's permission to make that call. Then his advice on how to handle it. There's a reason we aren't lawyers yet."

"You can't tell him." Jay shook his head and flashed a look of desperation. Whatever had been growing between them, he was pushing the chips to the middle of the table and betting it all on this moment. Did he matter to her already? Would she compromise herself after such a brief time together? "I'm asking you to give me more time. Please."

The urgency in his voice was unsettling. He'd been this laid-back guy she pegged as uncaring and a screwup. Now here he was, his eyes glassed over with the shadow of tears, begging her not to rat him out.

"Why?" She held her breath without realizing it, nearly to the point of being dizzy.

"We're going to call Mary-Lee's first husband." Jay cleared his throat and keyed a number into the phone on the table.

"No. I'm serious now, Jay. We are in over our heads, and I'm not going to get in trouble for this. Hang up the phone."

"Hello?"

"Hi." Jay blinked back some emotion. "It's me."

"Oh, Jay, how you doing?"

"Good. I just wanted to check in."

"Is the internship going all right?"

"It's harder than I thought." Jay rubbed at his temple. "I guess everything has been with law school."

"You'll do fine. Keep at it. Hey listen, I've got a conference call to jump on in five minutes. Can I call you later?"

"Yeah, of course. Oh, my friend is here with me. She wanted to say hi."

Vera felt like a deer frozen by oncoming headlights. "Uh, Hello."

"Hi, good to know Jay's making some friends. I'm Douglas Nielson."

"Vera Pedro," she stuttered out.

"Okay then, I've got to get going. I'll call you later, son."

"Bye, Dad." Jay disconnected the line and flopped down into the chair.

"I don't understand." Vera planted both hands on the table and stared at him. "Your father is Douglas Nielson, the first husband of Mary-Lee?"

"Yes."

"But your last name is Crawley?"

"It's my grandmother's maiden name. My father was worried that even with my name being redacted in the court records I'd have trouble. I went from Jeremy Nielson to Jay Crawley."

"You're Mary-Lee's first son?" The room seemed to spin like a carnival ride as Vera tried to go over every conversation they'd had up until this point. "You've been lying?"

"No." Jay shook his head. "I never lied to you."

"Oh I'm sorry, was I supposed to ask you directly if the woman convicted of killing her child was also your mother?"

"I can explain."

"No need." She tossed her hands up and made her way to the door. "This twisted little game just became a solo adventure. You do whatever you want, just do it somewhere else."

"Vera, please don't go. I can't do this on my own."

"You can't do this at all," she cut back. "There are advocacy groups that the families of the convicted can work with. But it's a huge conflict of interest for you to be involved in this on your own. You could nullify any findings, just by inserting yourself into this. Not to mention how twisted it is to play with people like this." She put her hand over her heart and felt for the dagger that must be there.

"I'm not trying to hurt anyone. I'm sorry if you feel like I misled you."

"I don't feel like you misled me. I know you tricked me. Now you go tell Michael your connection to this or I will."

"Vera, I want to help my mother. I'm never going to be a lawyer, do you understand that? I can't pass the bar. I've got ADHD, and I'm dyslexic. It's not that people with those things can't be lawyers, it's just I don't have what you have. I can't do it. But I have pushed myself this far so I could be in this moment. I know enough law and now have some resources to actually be able to do something."

"And what is it you want to do?"

"Get my mother out of prison. She didn't kill Pauly. I know she didn't."

"How?"

"Because if she loved him a fraction of how she loved me she couldn't hurt him. But if you go in right now and tell Michael, my only shot is gone."

"It's one law firm. You can go do this on your own. Find an innocence project who's interested."

"I've tried. None of them are. For all the reasons you said. People aren't sure they want to free a woman who might have killed a baby. They can't get right with that. This is my best shot. Here. Don't take that from me yet, please."

"You don't need to be here to do what you want." She twisted her face up in confusion.

"You're right," he agreed. "It's not about the location or even the resources Michael's offering. At first it was. I thought maybe I could pull a Hail Mary with that stuff. But then I met you. And that long shot, it actually became something I could see working. You are everything I'm not. If you were her child she'd be out already, but she got stuck with a kid like me who can barely follow the curriculum and has to take every bit of his energy to pass the exams. I know I've been a pain in your ass and you want nothing to do with me. But I need you."

"You what? Jay, this is insane. You hardly know me. I don't know you."

"If you can look me in the eye right now and say you don't feel something for me, even if it's pity, then fine. I'll walk away. I'll catch the bus to South Carolina and go back to having no chance in the world at helping my mother."

"I'm not a lawyer. I'm not equipped to help you."

"Vera." He closed the gap between them and took her hand in his. "This is not only about the law. It's about you. Who you are.

What you can accomplish when you set your mind to it. I need some of that right now."

Vera ran her hands over her face and groaned. "Why did you tell me the truth? You could have kept this up for a little while."

He drew in a sharp breath and brushed a hand across her flushed cheek. "I think when you lie to people it creates these spaces between you and them. It makes it hard to ever really get close. I know we just met. I'm probably being crazy, but if there's even the slightest chance that someday we could be close, I didn't want to wreck my shot at that."

Their lips were close, their breath ragged. "Don't you dare kiss me," Vera whispered, her voice shaking. "If you kiss me right now I'll assume you're only trying to get what you want. I'll figure you're playing me. You either want to kiss me or you want my help."

"I'm not trying to play you," he insisted. "I want both."

"You know how matter works. No two things can take up the same space at the same time. Decide which one you want."

"What do you want?" He licked his lips and ran his hand again over her cheek. She wanted to lean in. His kiss, the promise of it, drew her like metal to a magnet. But she wouldn't make that choice. It was too spontaneous. Reckless.

"I'll help you."

He nodded and reluctantly stepped back. "I'm screwing things up for you. I know how much you hate that. I'm sorry."

"Just keep your promise. You said by the end of the summer I'd be glad you were here."

"I'm not doing great so far. It's not even the end of the week and you're ready for me to go."

This time it was her who took his hand. "I'm not ready for you to go. We have work to do."

CHAPTER 11

"You called your dad this time, right?" Jay tucked his hands in his pockets as they walked up Betty's front steps.

"Yeah. He knows I'm having dinner here tonight." She stopped on the bottom step and lowered her voice. "Are you sure you don't want to tell Michael what's going on? He's a good man. I might have overreacted before. We can trust him."

Pins and needles crept up his spine. He'd put Vera in a terrible position and the guilt was tough to swallow. "It's not too late to change your mind. I can hop a bus back to my house and hang out there for the summer instead."

She slowly blinked at him. "No." Tucking her hair behind her ears, she searched for the right words. "The problem is I'm not exactly sure why I'm saying no. I'm worried it's because I don't want you leave." Her gaze darted away. "Which is absolutely crazy because we just met and every second we've been together you've annoyed me. Or infuriated me. I should be buying you your bus ticket home right now."

"Vera." He reached out and took her hand. "I know. I totally agree. It doesn't make sense. But I feel kind of the same way. Maybe we give it a little time and see what comes of it."

"No plan. Sounds like you."

"See, you know me pretty well already. But we don't have to do it my way. If you want to put this on a spreadsheet or something, I'm down. Just know I'm not trying to pressure you at all. Not to help me and not to . . ."

"What?"

He smiled, knowing it would get a rise out of her. "No pressure to fall head over heels for me."

She yanked her hand back and huffed. "You're pressing your luck." With clear intent she stepped up and brushed by him, dangerously close.

Jay hadn't been here for a family dinner yet. He'd been warned, but it couldn't do justice to what he was witnessing. Every flat surface, the kitchen table, the dining room table, and a coffee table in the living room had place mats and plates on it. Every burner on the stove had a pot simmering. The flood to his senses was more than he expected. There was a clamoring of voices and a tidal wave of delicious smells.

"I'm not going to have to put the cuffs on you again, am I?" Bobby asked, slapping Jay's back and chuckling.

"No," Jay answered, throwing his hands up disarmingly. "I'll behave myself."

Jules grabbed a stack of napkins to place at each table setting around the house. "That sounds like a good story. I look forward to hearing it. Piper, did you know your husband has been arresting Betty's houseguest?"

A dark-haired woman rolled her even darker eyes as she grabbed the full bread basket to take around to the tables. "Nothing surprises me any more with Betty's houseguests. They are always into something. Hey Vera sweetheart, how is your dad?"

"He's good," Vera replied with an edge of nervousness. So it was becoming clear, no robbing a bank with her. Luckily her dark skin didn't show much of a blush. "The shop is pretty busy. He's almost done with the starter in your car, Betty."

Effortlessly managing the stove, Betty gave a nod of approval. "I'll send a plate home to your father tonight. Give him my gratitude for working on the car so quickly and lending Jay something in the meantime."

Michael came in through the screen door and loosened his necktie. "You two have some explaining to do." He focused in on Vera and Jay with a stern look. From the corner of his eyes, Jay could see her about to crack. The pressure of disappointing someone was clearly too much for Vera. "You set the motion sensor alarm in the office even though it's the night the cleaning crew comes. That was a fun trip back there."

"Oh," Vera stammered. "I forgot. I can't believe I forgot. You told me this morning. That's not like me at all."

"Honey," Jules said, gently nudging her, "don't listen to him. It's much easier to find a way to convince him it was his fault."

Michael accepted the beer Bobby was handing him and shrugged. "She's right. You might get further in life if you intern for Jules instead. That's real sage advice she's giving you."

"Ignore him." Jules gave a sideways glance to her husband who broke into a full laugh. "The rest of us do."

Betty started handing out dishes heaped with food and pointing around to show where they should be placed. Jay watched like the new kid at summer camp. Everyone else already found their bunk and knew the songs.

"You're looking a little wide-eyed." Betty handed him a large glass pitcher of lemonade and pointed toward the living room. "Would you feel most comfortable at the kids' table?"

"Did you all choreograph this before I came? Is this a flash mob?" He stepped back as Jules and Piper balanced drinking glasses for everyone.

Betty smiled. "When you've been doing this as long as we

have, it's second nature. We switch off now between here and the restaurant."

"Speaking of which," Bobby said with a stern voice, "I thought you were supposed to be busing tables there to help out."

"He's starting this weekend." Betty pointed her wooden spoon threateningly at Bobby. "You have your own business to mind."

"I'm looking forward to it. I hear you're well fed if you're an employee."

Michael patted his back. "Just expect to buy a new belt."

Dinner was mostly filled with arguments. There was a new builder coming into town and hoping to put up condos where a historic building now stood. Some around the table were in favor of progress; others were upset at the lack of respect for history.

The debate ran right through dessert and as they all sat on the porch, it seemed to finally be winding down.

"It's a beautiful night," Vera said, stepping off the porch and looking up at the spattering of stars. "Not a cloud out there. There's a shooting star. Make a wish." The wonderment on her face drew Jay's eyes. For someone so serious, it was nice to see the childlike awe.

Betty's chair creaked as she rocked and hummed. "I wish this damn heat would break. My hair is as frizzy as a poodle in a sauna."

Though it seemed impossible with this group, silence crept in, broken only by the crickets. The minutes ticked by as Betty began to hum another tune, and eventually people started with their goodbyes.

Michael had an armful of something Betty was sending them home with as he offered Vera a ride. "We can drop you off on our way."

"I'll take her." Jay recognized his urgent tone and immediately tried to cover. "I don't mind. It's a nice night."

He was too late; everyone was already making faces and

nudging each other playfully. Now it was up to Vera to either tell him to bug off or accept his offer. If she accepted it was basically like telling everyone she wanted to spend time with him even when they had no real reason to. There would be teasing and knowing looks.

"Whatever," Vera said coolly. "I guess we can talk about the case. I did find an article I thought would be helpful."

Jay shrugged. "Yeah, that's what I was thinking too."

Betty stood off the porch and waved goodbye as she got one last joke in. "I'm sure that's what you were thinking. Good thing we can't read minds though. I think we'd be blushing."

He was pulling out of the driveway a few minutes later as Vera balanced the leftover food Betty had sent home for her father. "Thanks for the ride home."

"I don't think you'll owe me any thanks for a while. What you're doing is way more than I'll ever be able to repay."

"Does your mom know you're doing this?"

"She doesn't know me at all. I haven't talked to her since I was a little boy. I don't know how she'd feel about this."

"Wait." Vera's back straightened. "You don't talk to her at all? You've never heard her side of the story?"

"When I was young I was angry with her. When I was old enough to realize how things really work, I knew she wasn't given a fair chance. I wanted to do something. Then I knew I couldn't talk to her until I had something worth saying. Some good news."

Vera twisted her face up as something seemed to hit her. "You went to law school because of this? How hard have you had to work to get to this moment?"

"Very."

"I've never done anything like this before. I feel like we're in over our heads. Even if we interview people and discover something, then what?"

"Then we'll do exactly what we planned to before. We tell Michael, and he can hand it over to the people who can use it to help her. I know I'm asking a lot of you, Vera. At any time you can bail. I won't hold it against you."

Her brows were creased with worry, her lips sucked between her teeth. It was all he could do not to kiss her. But to blur the lines between them any more would be unfair. Instead he pulled the car up to her house and sat silently as she made a move to get out.

"You won't be mad if I don't help you?"

"No."

"But you won't get anywhere without my help."

He smiled. "Probably not. And it kills me to have to admit that after all the arguing we've done."

"Let's meet an hour early at the office tomorrow. That way we can use the database Michael has access to. We can track down people who knew your mother when she was young."

"See you then."

"One more thing," she said as she stood, and then leaned back into the car. "I like my coffee with two sugars and skim milk. A donut wouldn't hurt either."

Vera closed the car door and strolled up to her house as if propelled by sheer confidence. Damn. He should have kissed her.

CHAPTER 12

"There are new rules." Vera was up at the white board looking like the sexy fantasy version of a teacher. "You don't just pick up the phone and cold dial a potential witness. We need to plan it. I have leads on two of your mother's good friends. They'd have known her well when she was pregnant with Pauly. They must have some insight. But we need to be strategic."

"It's very cute when you take charge."

"It's pigheaded when you say stupid things like that."

Jay nodded his apology.

"I'm serious about this. We make our calls with a clear goal in mind. We can start with Susan Ikes."

"Start with what?" Michael asked, doing a great job of sneaking up dad-style.

"We're making a list of character witnesses who might be willing to speak on Mary-Lee's behalf." Vera closed a folder quickly and Jay rolled his eyes. She was awful at this.

"That's a good place to start. Can I give you some tips?"

"Please." Vera grabbed a pen.

"It's easy to think that because so much time has passed the emotion will be lessened some. I doubt it will. Situations like this stay with people. They remember more than you expect. It's important to treat them like their pain, if they have any, is relevant."

"Got it." Vera wrote the note down and waited for more.

Michael walked in and gently took the pen from her hand. "There won't be a test on this, Vera. This is the part of this job you can't learn about in a classroom. The people. Character witnesses for a woman sitting in prison for murdering a child. There will be layers you cannot imagine. Empathy will be crucial."

"Better let me do the talking," Jay joked, but Vera only glared back. "Kidding."

"I hear what you're saying, Michael. I'll do my best."

"Also," Michael said as he handed back the pen and made his way out of the room, "do not overpromise anything. We are not working this case. We are not filing any appeals. This is you doing a project. I doubt these folks have been called for over a decade. They're going to assume this means more than it does."

Jay leaned in. "But it could mean everything."

"I appreciate your enthusiasm and optimism. It's cute. You're like little dumb lawyer puppies. But you have a long way to go here. This is about five summers worth of work, and even that might not be enough. Just keep your expectations realistic."

Vera had waited patiently for her chance to rebut. "I guess that will be my department."

"Then you're a perfect pair." Michael had a devilish grin as he headed down the hallway.

"You know the rumors will fly soon about the two of us." Vera gave him a challenging look.

"I don't think I'd mind being associated with a woman like you. You'll help my new reputation in Edenville."

"That's not what you have to worry about. It's what happens if you screw up and hurt me in any way. It won't be taken lightly. I hope you aren't too attached to your knee caps."

"I do like them right where they are actually." He instinctively rubbed his hands over his knees.

"Keep that in mind when you don't follow my rules. Now, we're calling Susan Ikes. Let's make a plan."

His fingers hovered over the phone and a grin spread across his face. "You mean at this number right here? That's where we can reach her?"

"Don't you dare." The challenge was almost too much but somehow he resisted.

"We can do it your way. For this anyway."

"What's that supposed to mean?"

He winked. "There will be some things between you and me where I don't let you take control of every detail. Sometimes I'm going to surprise you."

"I hate surprises."

"I can promise you won't hate the kind of surprise I'm talking about."

CHAPTER 13

"Are you ready?" Vera gave Jay a long hard look. He didn't seem ready. "This is for real."

"Yes, I know. We've practiced the script a thousand times now. There's a chance you're overthinking this."

"You can't overthink something important."

"We're certainly putting that theory to the test."

"Dial."

"Is there a certain finger I should use to dial?" He was patronizing her, and it made her blood boil.

"How about this finger." She held up her middle finger and gave him a cross look.

"Dialing."

The phone rang three times and Vera held her breath. For some reason Jay didn't seem like he was terrified at all. He looked perfectly relaxed. Something Vera hadn't been since . . . she couldn't even remember.

"Hello?"

"Hi, is this Susan Ikes?" Jay asked, running his finger across the scripted paper to take a dig at Vera.

"It is."

"My name is Jay I'm calling on behalf of Cooper Jenkins and Moore Law firm. Do you have a minute to talk about the case I'm working on? I believe you were friends with the defendant."

Vera balled her hands into fists. That was not the script. He wasn't supposed to say he was working on a case or align himself with the law firm directly.

"What case?"

"You were friends with Mary-Lee Stevens."

"You're working on Mary-Lee's case? Really?"

"Not me alone, my team."

"Oh that's wonderful. If you don't mind the sound of my grandkids yelling in the background, I'm happy to talk."

It hit Vera as sad that Mary-Lee would never have a chance to meet her grandkids if Jay decided to have any.

"It's no problem at all. We're so grateful for your time. So you were friends with Mary-Lee?"

"Best friends."

"But you didn't testify on her behalf?"

"I couldn't. I wanted to, but her lawyer didn't want me going up there."

"Why?"

"It's not an easy thing for me to talk about."

Jay looked up and met Vera's concerned gaze. "Anything you can tell us would be very helpful for Mary-Lee."

"Her husband and I were, well, we had been together. Not in the sense that we were sleeping together. It wasn't really like that."

"How was it?"

"He was very tired from traveling, and Mary-Lee was exhausted from caring for a new baby that always seemed to be sick. I worked as a bartender and he used to come in and see me when things got tough. We'd talk."

"That's it?"

"He came in quite a bit to see me. Sometimes three or four times a week. He'd come straight from work and tell Mary-Lee he was stuck at the office. I knew it was wrong, but in my mind, back then, I thought I was being a good friend. We were all so young."

"But you never really did anything?"

"We kissed. Twice."

"And her lawyer felt like if you were on the stand that would hurt her case?"

"I guess."

Jay cleared his throat and attempted to right himself. "Forget all that for a moment. What kind of mother was she? What kind of person was she? If this wasn't an issue and you could have gotten on the stand, what would you have said?"

"Oh," her voice sang. "Mary-Lee would do anything for people she cared about. Too much, really."

"What do you mean?"

"Well, all the years I've had to reflect on it, I've realized Daryl wasn't fair to her. Not by a long shot. If my husband was out, sitting at a bar with my best friend while I was home, sleep deprived and overwhelmed, I'd kill him. Daryl had very high expectations of her, and I don't think that helped the situation. He would get mad if his dry cleaning wasn't picked up, even when Pauly wasn't feeling good. She was a good cook but dinner wasn't always on the table when he wanted it. I feel so much guilt that I would sit around and listen to him complain about this stuff. I just thought it was venting."

"Do you think—?"

Susan cut him off. "No, you know what, I'm not letting myself off the hook like that. I liked hearing him say this stuff. It made me feel better about myself. She was twice the woman I was. I was jealous of her. Him coming to see me made me feel superior. It wasn't until he kissed me that I knew I was on a slippery slope. I wouldn't be able to live with myself if it went any further."

"I understand." Jay leaned back in his chair and looked at the ceiling. "What made her a good woman? A good mother?"

"Now that I'm a mom, I know exactly what it was. Back then I'm not sure I could have really articulated it. Parenting has a lot to do with sacrifice. You have to give, and then when you think you have nothing left, you give more. That was Mary-Lee's super power."

"Her first son lived with his father." He hadn't posed a question. He couldn't seem to form a coherent one.

"That killed her. I can't tell you how often she cried about that. Before she was pregnant with Pauly, when she and I would go out and have some drinks, she would always show me pictures her ex-husband sent. Her son was a really happy boy. She knew it was the best place for him, but it always ended in tears."

"Did she explain why she felt it was the best place for him? By that point, she was remarried. She wasn't a single mother, her family was growing, why not update the custody agreement?"

Vera adjusted her posture enough to get his attention. Her look of worry seemed bigger than the fact that he'd left the script behind.

"So, at the beginning it was because her ex was more stable. And she really believed a boy needed his dad. The schools were good. The area was safer. It made more sense. She thought she would see him more, but it wasn't easy for her to travel back and forth. It cost more than she had most months. Once she was with Daryl I think she had concerns about how her boy would be accepted into the family they were building."

"Daryl would have had a problem with it?"

"He didn't like her having contact with her ex. She never had anything bad to say about him, and I remember Daryl making comments that if he was so great they should have stayed together. She liked to keep the peace, and her son was thriving with his father. It was the best thing for everyone."

"Everyone but her."

"Yes."

"Do you think she hurt Pauly?"

The silence gave Jay time to finally decipher Vera's expression. She thought he was being selfish. That this was more about getting answers for himself than the case.

"I can't answer that." Susan sniffled. "I know if I were in her shoes, a sick kid, my husband always gone and always demanding something of me, I might want a way out. When my second daughter was born she had these terrible ear infections. My oldest was still in diapers. I didn't think I was going to make it. And I had loads of help. My parents. My husband. Those long nights, I would close my eyes and think about Mary-Lee. I didn't want to hurt my child, but you're half out of your mind. I know that Mary-Lee loved both her children, and she'd run through fire to give them the best she could. The only way I could see it happening is if she snapped. And I thought maybe she would shake him or something. Putting antifreeze in his bottle, I can't see her doing that."

"Is there anything else you want to add?" Jay scratched down a few more notes.

"Do you think you'll get her another trial? This time I'd really like to speak on her behalf. I have so many stories about how wonderful she is."

"Have you kept in touch?"

"I tried to but all my letters were sent back to me. I'd imagine she found out about Daryl and me. She had every right to cut me out."

"I appreciate your time."

"When will there be an appeal? I'd like to stay up to date on what's going on." The urgency in Susan's voice was genuine.

Vera shook her head. He knew he couldn't promise anything. Michael had been clear about that.

"We'll be in touch." He said his goodbyes as Vera sighed with relief. When the line disconnected she looked ready to pounce but softened suddenly.

"Are you all right?" She gave him a look of understanding, surprising him completely.

"You're not mad?"

"It's your mom." That was it in a simple answer. There was so much more that could be said. Yet somehow she knew those three little words summed it up best.

"Yeah. I'm all right."

CHAPTER 14

"Daddy, I need your advice." Vera ducked down to the side of the car her father was working on.

"I've only had to wait twenty-something years to hear those words. Are you saying my headstrong, know-it-all daughter, actually wants my advice?"

"I did thirty seconds ago." He rolled out from under the car and wiped his greasy hands on the red rag he pulled from his pocket.

"Spill it." His warm dark eyes were filled with love. "I'm listening."

"It's always been really easy for me to tell right from wrong. I'm not saying I've always done the right thing, but it's not usually confusing to me. What do you do when you're not sure?"

He leaned against the old rusty car and smiled. "I'm not going to get details am I?"

"No."

"All right, well I have over twenty years of advice for you that I've been saving up so I should be able to figure something out. Let's see. How to decide what is right when it's not completely obvious. I've been in this situation."

"And what do you do?"

"I ask myself the big three questions."

"Dad." She rolled her eyes but he waved her off.

"I'm serious. I ask myself, is someone in imminent physical danger? Will this choice impact people I love in a bad way that I could have prevented, even if it was at my own expense?"

"And the third?"

"Will my dad be disappointed in me?" He couldn't help but laugh that corny chuckle he reserved for the punch line of his dad jokes.

"You were so close to being serious."

"I am being serious." He put a hand on her shoulder. "The only thing that blurs the difference between right and wrong is our emotions. Sometimes we let fear confuse us. Sometimes we let our feelings for someone mess with our decisions."

"And that's so bad?"

"If you take them out of the equation and the answer would be perfectly clear, that's something to consider. You can tell me the details, you know. You can trust me with that."

"I know I could, Daddy. I just think I need to sort this out on my own. It's not nearly as dramatic as I'm making it sound right now. I want to make sure I'm thinking clearly."

"You mean even when you're looking in those dreamy eyes of that new guy in town? Are you all dizzy and overtaken by butterflies when he says your name?" He clapped his hands in a silly way.

"And the moment is over." She leaned in and kissed his cheek, taking in the familiar smell of his overalls, a mix of their laundry detergent and motor oil.

"Have you started writing his name all over your notebook?" She was halfway out of the large bay door while he kept shouting jokes.

"Did you start planning your wedding? You had better be wearing white."
"Bye, Daddy."
"Bye, girl."

CHAPTER 15

"What are you doing here?" Vera slid her bedroom window open and whispered down to Jay. He'd been throwing little pebbles at her window until she opened up.

"I think he did it."

"What? What are you talking about?"

"Come down. I need to talk to you."

"It's two in the morning. I'm in my pajamas."

He took a few big steps back to try to see her better on the second floor. "What kind of pajamas?"

"Shut up. If my dad hears you out here you'll be sorry."

"Then come down. We need to talk." There was just enough slur in his voice to tell her he'd been drinking.

"You're drunk? You show up at my window at two in the morning drunk? Trust me, you have me confused with someone else. I'm no booty call. Now if you try a couple doors down, Old Widow Warder is a bit handsy, she might be interested."

"Vera, I would never booty call you. Ever." He looked wounded by her accusation, and it stung her.

"Well then what are you doing here?"

"I think I figured something out about the case, and it couldn't wait until the morning. I had to share it with you."

"Fine. I'll change and be right down. But I'm telling my dad we're going to be outside. Wait, how did you get here?"

"I walked."

"From where?"

"The bar. I don't know, a few miles I guess."

"You left the car there?"

"Yes.," he said as though it was obvious. "I'm drunk."

"Didn't you think of that before you got drunk?"

A voice bellowed out from the window next to hers. "Obviously he didn't intend on getting drunk when he sat down. Good on you, son, for not drinking and driving. Now my daughter is going to come downstairs then be back in her bed in the next twenty minutes. Isn't she?"

"She is." Jay nodded vigorously.

"Then you are going to sleep on our couch. And while you are lying there you will remember that I have lived in this apartment a long time. I know which floorboards creak between that couch and my daughter's room."

"Yes sir."

"Vera, go talk to the boy. He walked miles to get to you."

"Daddy." She ground her teeth together but finally gave in. "I'll be right down."

She hurried around her room. She ran a brush through her hair. Tossed on her best-looking yoga pants and swapped her holey college sweater for a cute workout shirt. She had no makeup on, but it would be crazy to put some on now. Right? That would be desperate. Silly. It didn't matter what he thought of her.

After a moment or two of arguing with herself, she settled for two quick swipes of mascara and Chap Stick, one with a little bit of tint. She rolled her eyes and grabbed a tissue to wipe it off.

Then decided to leave it. He was making her head spin and that was not going to work.

She marched down with purpose. This chaos could not be a part of her life. Middle of the night drunk chat out her window would not work for her.

As she swung open the door she readied to launch into some speech about having some decent manners. But he didn't give her a chance to speak.

"It's Daryl. I know it was him."

"What?"

"Daryl hurt Pauly. It had to be him. Think about it. He made a move on my mother's best friend. He was a liar. He wanted out of his life, obviously." He braced one hand on the stair railing and looked desperately at her.

"He was traveling the night they checked him into the hospital. I think he was only home a few hours. He said Pauly was already sick when he arrived."

"Sure, that's what he said. What we didn't know was how long it would take for symptoms to show up. If he poisoned him with antifreeze, it can take as little as thirty minutes before signs appear. It could have been him."

"But he didn't make any visits to Pauly at the hospital. Only your mother did. He died there a day after her visit." Her voice crept across the truth, knowing it would wound him.

"No, you're not thinking broadly enough. There are ways he could have gotten around that. I mean ask yourself, why didn't he have any visits with his own son in the hospital? Doesn't that strike you as odd?"

She licked her lips, tasting the stupid gloss she'd put on, and realizing now how dumb that seemed. "I think we should explore this theory in the morning. I'll be more rested. You'll be sober. My father won't be gripping a baseball bat, counting down the minutes on his watch."

"He did this, Vera. I'm telling you." He raised one hand and planted it on her shoulder. With a small stumble, he leaned in close.

"Don't kiss me." She leaned back and narrowed her eyes. "Don't show up in the middle of the night drunk and kiss me. Not like this."

"I wasn't going to kiss you." He blinked slowly, the way only a drunk person could. That long attempt to get the world to stop spinning. "But I could maybe use a hug."

His head dropped down, weathered by the night and the revelations. She was certain he was probably wrong. The odds that Daryl had hurt his child with poison were low. It didn't fit the profile of a father's murder. Sadly those were more physical and violent. It was a mother who would usually find some distant way to end her child's life.

As he fell into her arms, that didn't seem to matter. His chin settled into her neck, and she could feel him drawing strength and breathing her in.

"I'm sorry I came here in the middle of the night." His words were a whisper through her hair. "I wasn't trying to make things complicated."

"My father is going to start turning the porch light on and off if we don't go inside." Reluctantly she let him go. He felt so good against her and his absence as they parted left an ache in her chest.

She settled him onto the couch and pulled a blanket over him. "We're going to get her out." His eyes were closed, and his lips turned up into a smile. "This is really going to happen. With you helping we can do this."

Her heart sank like a rock tossed into the sea. She brushed his hair back off his forehead and listened as his breathing got steady and slow.

Her father's voice wasn't much of a shock. She had heard him coming down the hall and stopping in front of the living room. "So this is your big conundrum?"

"Yeah."

"He seems to think you've got some special powers."

"He's just drunk and confused." She shook her head and looked at the now completely passed out Jay. "I'll set him straight tomorrow."

"Or?"

"Or what?"

"Sometimes we rise to the expectation someone else puts on us. Sometimes we surprise even ourselves."

"You don't really know what you're suggesting. It's a very serious situation. In the long run he's going to be heartbroken. I'm not going to be able to protect him from that."

Her father nodded and leaned against the doorframe. "None of us can really stop a heartbreak. But we can always help put it back together. I say stick with him. If you can't get him what he wants, at least be what he needs."

"When did you get so smart?" She shook her head. "No, a better question is when did you start rooting for the men in my life?"

"You haven't given me much to pick from. This one seems like he at least has some basic human emotions. That's a step up."

She slapped his shoulder playfully and accepted the hug he offered. "Just follow your heart."

"When does that ever work out?"

"It's how I got you."

CHAPTER 16

When she woke, there was a brief moment when Vera forgot Jay was asleep on her couch. It was just another morning. But then a flash of her father loudly brewing coffee had her jumping up. Surely albums loaded with embarrassing baby pictures would soon be passed around. She threw on some clothes and rushed down the hall.

The kitchen was quiet. The couch was empty. She was alone. The note on the fridge was her father's familiar scribble.

Took your friend back to his car. He'll pick you up for work after he goes and apologizes to Betty for making her worry. Love, Dad.

She checked the clock on the wall and decided she should get ready. Sleeping hadn't magically helped her find perspective or answers. She and Jay weren't doing this for the same reason. His personal connection to the case would cloud his judgment. Recklessness had no place in the legal system. In the long run he could do more damage to his mother's case. He could jeopardize Michael's firm. Hurt his reputation. And there was the matter of her own future. This summer was meant to be the foundation for the rest of her life. The solid ground she could build something on. Now suddenly it felt like quicksand.

For most of the next hour she debated herself. It didn't feel right to abandon him either. It had been a long time since Vera had felt a pull toward someone as intense as what she felt for Jay.

When a car horn beeped out front she felt a buzz of excitement seeing him lean out the driver side window. As she took her first few steps toward the car she could see a wild look in his eyes.

"I'm going down to see him."

"Who?"

"Daryl. I can drop you off at Michael's office first. I plan to be back tonight but maybe not in time to pick you up."

"Michael is expecting us both in the office today. You can't just hop in a car and drive to another state. Not to mention that car is a loaner from my dad. Betty's car will be finished tomorrow. Maybe we can plan something over the weekend. I can even go with you."

"I'll call Michael later today. I'm telling you it'll be worth the trip. I know there is more to Daryl's story, and I think looking him in the eye is going to make the difference. I already asked your father this morning if he minded if I had the car out most of the day today and he said it was fine."

"You think Daryl is just going to admit he was the one who hurt Pauly? This isn't the movies. People don't confess because you ask nicely."

"I didn't say I was going to ask nicely." She hoped his face would break into a smile, but it didn't. "Come on, I'll drop you off at the office."

"No." She shook her head and sucked her lip between her teeth. "The smart thing to do is go into the office, talk to Michael, and explain the whole truth. He'll know what to do."

"I appreciate why you're saying that. In your experience,

that's how this works. My dad is not like your dad. My friends are not like Betty. I've done things on my own most of my life."

"But now you have people like that in your life. Why not take advantage of it? Everyone here will understand where you are coming from. They'll want to help you. But if you blow off work today and go on a wild goose chase, you'll be pushing away the people who could help." She rested her hands on the frame of the car window, as if she could hold him there and change his mind.

"Let me give you a ride to the office." His eyes weren't bleary and tired like they were last night. They were determined and resolute. She had to admire his convictions.

"If you insist on going, I'll go with you."

"No." He shook his head and gripped the steering wheel tightly. "You're not getting mixed up with this. Your head would explode if you thought you were disappointing people. I can't do that to you."

"You don't think I would be helpful on this trip?" She propped her hand up on her hip.

"Of course you would be."

"Then I'm coming. But on one condition."

His expression went from excited to skeptical. "I knew this was too good to be true."

"When we get back, no matter what happens, you tell Michael the truth. You can trust him."

He sized her up, his eyes running up one side of her and down the other as he considered the terms of this agreement. "Trust is a very obscure concept. It requires blind faith. I'm surprised you can get your mind around it."

"I have good people around me. Now you do too. I'm coming with you today because I trust that you're not going to get us in any kind of real trouble. When we get back, you trust me that you can count on Michael."

Jay nodded and reached across to unlock the passenger side door. "You sure about this?"

Her brain shouted no. But there was a flutter in her heart that drowned it out. "Maybe it's time to take a chance."

"Because you trust me?" There was a fleeting look of worry on his face as though he knew her trust might be misplaced.

"If I'm being honest, maybe I'm just worried about what might happen to you if I don't go."

He nodded as though that answer made more sense. She climbed into the passenger seat and glanced at her cell phone. They could still make it to the office if she wanted to. He would take her there. He wouldn't say a word.

"Last chance." He was reading her mind.

"South Carolina?"

"South Carolina."

CHAPTER 17

He still couldn't believe she came. But she was close enough to touch. Out of the corner of his eye he'd catch a glimpse of her hair whipping in the wind as they cruised down the highway. If there was no underlying reason for their road trip he'd actually be happy right now. Having a woman like Vera in the passenger seat for a road trip was like a fantasy. Pit stops. Snacks. Singing to songs on the radio. It was summer at its finest. But that was the pretend part.

She must be freaking out inside. It had been two hours since she sent a text to her father and left a voicemail for Michael. It was a stuttering mess of an explanation about a lead on the case and a road trip to South Carolina, punctuated by enough apologies to choke an elephant. She'd gotten a text back from Michael but didn't tell him exactly what it said.

"Only a couple hours." He was trying to make her feel better, but there was really no way for him to do that. "I have his work address so I figure we can talk to him there."

"Are you going to tell him who you really are?" The words felt like a blow to his chest. It wasn't that he was trying to lie about who he was. This was just easier. Less messy. Look how it had already changed things between them.

"You make it sound like I'm in witness protection." He punctuated it with a laugh but she didn't seem to find it funny.

"I'm just wondering exactly what I'm getting myself into. You're about to accuse a man of murder while he's at his job. That's with no evidence. No authority to do so. I'm starting to think my biggest help will be providing bail money for you."

"Let's say I'm willing to take another approach. What do you suggest?" He turned the radio down and forced his mouth closed. He would listen. Vera was brilliant. She cared enough about him to get in this car even with all the drama it would bring to her life.

"I've been reading his witness statements." She licked her lips and turned her body partly toward him in the passenger seat. It was hard to stay focused on anything when she looked like summertime and smelled like heaven. "In all of his interviews, he seems to speak with a level of detachment about Pauly. Mary-Lee is distraught. She's overwhelmed and even self-critical of her skills as a mother. Daryl is matter of fact. He calls Pauly *him* or *he* more than by his name, almost like he can't say it. The police list him as cooperative."

"I'm telling you, in my gut I know he did this."

"Technically the timeline doesn't exclude him. If this were poisoning by antifreeze, he wouldn't have had to be home long for it to impact Pauly. But remember Pauly was deemed a *sick kid*. His short nine months were plagued with illness similar to the symptoms of the poisoning that killed him. We'd have to know where Daryl was each of those times. We have his pediatrician's records. We know when she brought him in. It's the most definitive way to eliminate him."

"Ah," Jay shook his head. "I'm not trying to exclude him. I'm trying to show he did this. He had motive and opportunity. Introducing that possibility could grant my mother a new case. Then a good lawyer could create doubt in the jury."

"And a good prosecutor would do exactly what I just said. She'd check where Daryl was each time Pauly was ill. If he was gone then your theory falls apart."

"You sound like that's what you're rooting for." The bite to his voice was impossible to miss, but equally impossible for him to hide.

"I'm on your side, Jay. That's why I'm here." She put her hand on his arm and squeezed gently. The touch was more centering than a month of quiet meditation. Not that he could manage more than thirty seconds of meditation. He felt like he'd been waging this war alone for so long and finally, over the crest of the hill, reinforcements had come.

"Thanks." It was all he could manage, but he could tell by the flutter of her eyelids she understood.

"But you have to tell me something. Your mother left you with your father because she thought it was the best place for you. When I hear you talk about home and your family, it doesn't seem like it turned out that way."

She wasn't wrong to assume that, and she wasn't over the line in asking. Vera deserved as much truth as he could give. "My dad is an amazing father. Just not to me. I have three half-siblings who came along when I was in that rebellious and annoying stage boys tend to go through."

"It's a long stage."

"You bet it is. My brothers and sister are great kids. My step mom isn't a monster. She's nice. But they formed a family. A real one. Maybe it was me trying to hold on to something that never really existed or maybe it was them feeling like I was the extra puzzle piece that never fit. I don't think they're bad people. I just think they aren't my people."

"You think that's why you want your mother out so badly? She'll be your person?"

"Maybe."

"I get it. I think sometimes what it would have been like if my father remarried and had more children. We are so close; it's just the two of us." She took the locket around her neck between two of her fingers and slid it mindlessly up and down the chain it sat on.

"That's from him?"

"Yes. It was his mother's."

"You think he'll be mad about all this?"

"I'm not sure. I've never done anything like it before. Skipping out on a responsibility to do something like this, that's new for me."

"I'm glad you came." Because risks seemed like a critical part to his life now, he took another one. Slipping his hand into hers, he laced their fingers together. Her soft skin was cool against his warm hand. A love song came on the radio and they both hummed along. If only this were just a road trip. If only things were simple.

CHAPTER 18

Sweat dripped down her tingling back. Vera was not built for lying. She had a professor who warned her that being a lawyer often required untruths and misdirection. She, however, was not convinced it was a prerequisite. Surely you could let the law guide you while holding on to your integrity.

"I'm here to see Daryl Stevens." She tipped her chin up and tried to look as though she belonged in this massive lobby with marble floors and grumpy looking security guards.

The woman behind the high receptionist desk waved toward the elevator and grunted. "Eighth floor." Her perfectly manicured nails slid a visitor pass across the counter, and Vera tried not to snap it up too eagerly.

"Thank you."

"That was easy," Jay remarked as he walked to catch up with her.

"I'm sure once we get to his floor someone is going to ask us if we have an appointment. I'm going to say no, and they're going to tell us to leave." She pressed the elevator button and clipped the badge to her shirt.

"You're clever. I'm sure you'll think on your feet." He nudged her gently and gave that devilishly charming smile. There was no telling what she would do to see a smile like that more often.

When the elevator doors opened, she drew in a deep breath as though when stepping off she'd find a lack of breathable air.

"Can I help you?" A slim woman with thick black curls smiled her red lipstick smile at them.

"We're here to see Daryl Stevens." Vera's voice stayed strong as she showed the visitors badge to the woman.

"Sure. He's finishing up with a client. He'll be walking them out any minute. You can catch him then. Just have a seat."

"Thanks," she said, clearing her throat. "Thank you."

They took a seat in the plush chairs and didn't say a word. Vera's heart pounded. What would they say when Daryl rounded the corner with his clients and the receptionist with her flowing silk shirt and kind eyes announced them?

"That's him," Jay whispered and Vera nodded. He looked exactly as he did on the company website.

When the two women in suits were in the elevator, the receptionist chimed in. "Mr. Stevens, these two are here to see you. Do you have time?"

"Sure." Daryl crossed the small lobby and met them with a handshake. "Come on back to my office."

Her mind spun as she wondered why no one had stopped them. No one even asked who they were or what they wanted.

"Have a seat." Daryl gestured for them to sit down in the large chairs tucked in the corner of his office. He leaned against his desk and clasped his hands. "What can I do for you?"

"Well, uh," Vera stuttered, "my name is Vera and this is Jay."

"Nice to meet you both. Are you here for an interview?"

"Technically," Vera cleared her throat, "we didn't have an appointment."

"That's all right. I leave my afternoons open so we have time to meet with non-profits and journalism students."

"Why?" Vera asked.

"You're not journalism students?" His brows furrowed as his concern seemed to grow. "I'm piloting a new program for a media outlet, and it's been drawing a lot of attention. I gave up trying to fit everyone in for appointments so we just do it on a first come, first served basis. But that's not why you're here?"

"We spoke on the phone," Jay interrupted, "about Mary-Lee's case."

Vera watched Daryl's face and tried to employ everything she'd learned in class regarding body language and facial cues. Did his eye twitch? Did his back tighten?

"Well then, what can I do for you? I told you everything I could think of on the phone. The rest you could find in the court records." His posture shifted as he folded his arms across his chest. Clearly discussing the launch of his media platform was more comfortable than discussing his late son.

"We have a few questions about your work travel." Vera pulled her bag to her lap and started pulling out papers.

"What will that do?" Daryl rounded his desk and sat down. "Don't get me wrong, I want to help in any way I can."

Vera could feel Jay's tension growing, and as he opened his mouth to speak, she braced herself.

"We want to validate that you were traveling each time Pauly was sick. It's important to Mary-Lee's case to be able to do that."

"The good news is that will be easy." Daryl clicked his keyboard and brought his computer to life. "I worked for a very small equity firm, and my travel was all reimbursed to me. Our tax records from the time would show when I traveled, where, and for how long. I'll have my accountant fax them over now."

"That would be great," Vera chirped, trying to sound cheerful.

"What else can we do? I really appreciate you all coming out and working hard for Mary-Lee. Like I said, I have a lot of guilt about that time and how I let her push me away after she was convicted. Maybe if I'd have stayed connected to her I could have helped sooner."

Vera cut in before Jay could. "We spoke with Susan Ikes. She said she didn't testify because there was concern over how it might have made your relationship with Mary-Lee look."

Daryl dropped his head down. "I knew there would be a chance she'd have something to say about it. She's right. I was an ass. Like I said, I take a lot of blame for leaving Mary-Lee on her own so much. Not only was she alone physically, but emotionally I was out of my depth. I was young and stupid."

Jay leaned in a little. "If these travel dates don't line up with Pauly's bouts of sickness, you understand you may become a suspect in his death."

Jay. Oh Jay. Don't.

Vera felt her back tingle with anxiety. This was not how it was supposed to go.

"What he means is—"

"I know what he means." Daryl leaned back in his chair. "And he's right. I always wondered why the police weren't looking into me more. They homed in on Mary-Lee right away. They got in my head and convinced me she'd done it. I'm telling you now I didn't hurt my son, but if it wasn't Mary-Lee they certainly didn't do enough to find that out. That's why the interest of your law firm is a welcome turn of events. I'll do anything to help. I mean that."

That didn't seem to appease Jay. "Even if it means you become a suspect?"

"I have nothing to hide."

"Besides the fact that you were making the moves on her good friend and lying about where you were most nights?" There was an escalating urgency in his voice like a fire following a line of gasoline back to the source, where it would all explode.

Daryl raised an eyebrow in his direction. "Have I done something to offend you? I've been quite blunt about my feelings here. I'm being transparent in providing you with whatever I can. It would be easy to follow my lawyer's advice from years ago and not discuss it with you or anyone else at all. This isn't going to be pleasant for me if this story ends up back in the news. My children could even find out. But it's all worth it to me. So tell me, what am I doing to piss you off?"

"We had a long ride here," Vera said quickly. "And we have a long ride back. I don't think Jay means to be so short. We've spent a good amount of time reading through the case, and it feels very personal to us."

"It's personal to me." Daryl drew in a deep breath. "How old are you two anyway? You seem like kids. What law firm is it you're working for? I'll be shocked if they have you two running around tossing out accusations like this. What's the name?"

Jay answered confidently. "Cooper Jenkins and Moore Law firm, I can assure you that we are not kids. We're going to chase down every lead, every angle until we know what really happened to Pauly."

Daryl's face twisted with confusion. "You're absolutely certain it wasn't Mary-Lee?"

"We are." Jay stood and loomed his six feet, three inches over the desk. "When should we expect your travel records?"

"In the next few minutes. If you wait by my receptionist, I'll have her get the fax over to you."

"That would be great." Vera was out of her chair, shaking his hand and chasing Jay out the door. "We appreciate your time."

"Keep me posted," Daryl pleaded.

Vera caught up with Jay and made sure he knew she was serious. "I'll meet you at the car."

"I can wait with you," he offered, but it was clear his mind was somewhere else.

"Go."

"I'm sorry if—"

"Go, Jay. I'll be right down."

When the elevator doors closed between them she finally felt the squeezing pressure release from her chest. There was physical distance between Jay and Daryl now and somehow that felt better.

The receptionist bounced over to Vera with a bubbly smile. "Mr. Stevens asked me to pass these along to you. Is there anything else you need? A drink? Some snacks for you and your friend?"

"We're fine, thank you." Vera took the folders and put them in her bag. "I really appreciate your help today."

"Any time. I have a feeling things around here are about to get very exciting." The receptionist was obviously talking about the upcoming changes from launching the new media platform. But maybe there would be a different kind of excitement that would sweep through Daryl's office.

CHAPTER 19

"Doesn't that make you want to puke?" Jay watched her in the passenger seat as she collated the tax records against Pauly's medical records.

"There are three instances where Pauly had sick visits at the doctor when Daryl was in town, though he didn't attend the doctor's appointments. The symptoms seem consistent with the ones that landed him in the hospital, just less severe."

"That's great."

"Why is that great? There are still nine other sick visits where he was out of town. He would have had no opportunity to administer any kind of poison to Pauly. A prosecutor would tear this theory apart."

"It's still something." Jay tapped his fingers on the steering wheel and tried to sound upbeat. But she was pissed. This was becoming a trend. He pushed the limits; she got swept up in his mess.

"It's really not, Jay. We drove all the way here so you could look him in the eye? Did you see anything? Because to me he sounded as accommodating and helpful as he did on the phone. I'm sure we could have asked him to fax these tax documents right to us at Michael's office. Instead we've pissed him off and made sure he believes we're working on behalf of Michael's law firm which we are technically not."

"I did see something in his eyes." Jay swallowed hard. "There is more to his story. Something he isn't saying."

"You know what doesn't get your mother a new trial? A gut hunch." She highlighted a few lines on the copies of medical records.

"What are you highlighting?" He leaned over to see but she shooed him away.

"Watch the road. I'm not sure what I'm looking at yet. I want to summarize his symptoms and the timeline of his illness to see if I can find a pattern. The family pediatrician testified, but I read her testimony and it had far more to do with how Mary-Lee seemed at each appointment than it had to do with Pauly. She made mention of his symptoms and she believed it was colic at first. Then a virus. She hardly had anything to say about why she never had his blood work done or why she didn't suspect poisoning."

"What are you getting at?" Jay tried to put the pieces in place but didn't see the point she was making. What would this have to do with Daryl?

"After eleven sick visits in nine months, a pediatrician should have been doing more than sending them home with tips on how to get through a stomach bug. I know it was decades ago but there were no tests for allergies. No blood work at all."

"But if it was poisoning?"

"She could have caught it earlier, before he was given a lethal dose. She was the closest doctor to Pauly's care, and it never crossed her mind that Mary-Lee would be the cause. All of her notes state that Mary-Lee seemed overly concerned with the baby's health and list her as a caring mother."

"How does this help?"

"It's context. It's part of a whole picture. You have a doctor who missed the opportunity to step in. You have a mother who is exhausted and brought this child in over and over again. I think we need to understand Munchausen syndrome better. This might have been something she was doing chronically, reaching out for help."

"I thoroughly researched the topic of Munchausen by proxy. She doesn't fit the profile."

"Does Daryl?"

"No."

"The fact is there is a baby who is chronically ill and a mother who continues to seek medical attention for him."

"I think maybe this was a mistake." Jay focused on the road as his blood pressure started to rise. The sun was starting to dip low and they were about an hour from Edenville.

"The trip? Or my help?"

"It's nothing personal, Vera. I just don't think we're pulling in the same direction. I'm not looking to understand why my mother hurt Pauly; I'm going to prove she didn't. I should have known that wouldn't be how you'd process this."

"You mean with logic and the law?"

"I mean inside the box. The same way everyone did the first time. I'll drop you off at home and apologize to your dad. I'll tell him it was my fault. Then I'll let Michael know I'm done too. I was wrong. This is not the solution."

"Jay"—she reached her hand out and touched the back of his neck gently—"you aren't getting rid of me and you aren't backing out on our deal. I went with you. Now you're going to talk to Michael about what's going on. After dropping the name of his law firm to someone you just accused of murder, you owe him an explanation."

"It won't matter if I'm taking off anyway." He shrugged and

leaned in to her touch. Her fingernails danced along the collar of his shirt.

"You aren't leaving. You aren't giving up."

"I'm not?"

"No."

"Why is that?"

She leaned across the center console and kissed his cheek, her hand still planted on the back of his neck. She trailed a few kisses down to his chin, and it took every ounce of his willpower not to turn his head to kiss her full on. Damn the road and its need to be watched while driving. "I want you to stay." Her lips hovered above his ear as she whispered to him. "Please don't go."

CHAPTER 20

"Well look what the cat dragged in." Betty was sitting at the counter of her restaurant as she counted out the cash drawer. "Michael, your degenerate employees have returned from their escapades."

"It was my fault," Jay began and Vera was grateful for his attempt, even though she was as much to blame as he was.

But Betty laughed. "Of course, it was your fault. Vera has been a levelheaded, arrow-straight, reliable member of this community all her life. It would take a wild boy like you to sway her from her responsibilities."

"That's not quite what happened," Vera tried, but Jules cut in.

"Oh no, it's too late. He's already corrupted her. They're probably going to spin out of control and turn into some crime duo crossing the country and causing havoc wherever they go."

Piper and Bobby were in the same booth as Michael and Jules, and Vera could tell they were having a good time at her expense. Luckily the rest of the Wise Owl was empty for the evening.

"I was wondering if I could talk with you, Michael." Jay had his hands tucked in his pockets and his head tilted to the side.

"Did you want to tell me that your name is Jeremy Neilson? That you're Mary-Lee's oldest son from her first husband?"

Vera felt the tires in her brain screeched to a stop. She was a step behind Jay and couldn't read his expression but surely he was as shocked.

"Ah, yeah."

"I already know that." Michael dropped his napkin onto his plate and stood. "Were you just here for your own agenda?"

"No, that's not it at all." Jay cleared his throat and Vera felt the overwhelming urge to come to his defense. But with what argument?

"Wait, how did you know?" Jay scratched at his head as he tried to figure out how his secret had been uncovered.

"I'm a smart guy." Michael paced around him with a funny grin. "First, you knew way too much about the case too quickly. Vera is much smarter than you, and she should have smoked you when I gave you the opportunity to pick a case. Second, no one comes to Edenville to intern at a law firm just because. Vera is here because it's home for her. Once I read the case files and saw that Mary-Lee had an older son who moved to the town you happen to be from, it was pretty easy to put together from there."

Betty tucked the money from the register in a bank deposit bag and hummed her disapproval at the whole situation. "No pie for you tonight, son." She rounded the corner and grabbed a pot of hot coffee. "But you can have coffee and the leftover fried chicken if you want it."

Betty was never all that good at withholding food as a form of punishment.

"We're starving," Vera admitted as she took a seat on a bar stool and tried to look pathetic. It wasn't hard. They'd been in the car most of the day, and she knew she looked like a hot mess.

Jay sat down next to her and clearly knew pathetic was the

way to go. He painted on the same expression and gratefully accepted the plate Betty gave.

"So kids," Michael said, walking around the other side of the bar and eyeing them both, "what do you have to say for yourselves?"

"Sorry?" Vera tried but she knew how hollow it sounded. "I mean I apologize for skipping out on work today. You know how much this internship means to me, and I didn't mean to jeopardize it."

"Don't blame her at all. I convinced her to come with me."

Piper laughed, "Yes, we all know how weak-minded and impressionable our little Vera can be."

"I didn't mean that." Jay filled his mouth with fried chicken and looked to Vera to rescue him.

She cleared her throat and gave it her best try. "I think anyone in this place can agree Jay has a good reason for what he's doing. Any of us would want to do the same."

Bobby finally chimed in. He was clearly on duty but had stopped for a break. "Of course we would want to help our mother if we could. But I'm not sure I'd go through the process of getting into law school to try to do it."

"It was the best I could think of. I needed knowledge, allies, and an opportunity. I'm sorry if I made any of you feel used in that process."

Michael nodded. "You literally used my law firm and my name to further your cause. I'm not sure it's a leap for me to feel used."

"Yeah that part was stupid," Jay admitted. "I told Vera though, I'll shove off after tonight. I'm not going to cause a bunch more problems for everyone. I'll catch a bus back home."

"Was there something there?" Michael asked, directing his question at Vera, not Jay. Her heart skipped a beat. Was he asking if there was something between them? "With the case," he clarified. "Was there something there in your opinion?"

She thought on it for a moment. "I don't think we have the whole picture, and at a minimum I think jury selection and hysteria over filicide at the time played a key role in her conviction. I don't believe her counsel acted with her interests in mind. Also I think advancements in science could play a key role in the case now."

"Look at her," Betty said, gently slapping Michael's shoulder. "If this boy doesn't ruin her, I think she's got a bright future."

"I won't ruin her." Jay looked at Vera fondly and gave a little grin. "She might wreck me though."

"What came of the little road trip today?" Michael still seemed skeptical but he was at least willing to hear them out. Jay was smart enough to let Vera do the talking; they'd be nicer to her for sure.

"Daryl Stevens provided his travel receipts and we compared them to Pauly's medical records to see if he was ever present when Pauly was sick."

"He was sick often?" Piper asked, all of them now coming up to the bar and gathering around.

Vera fished out some files and opened them. Apparently they had been forgiven, and everyone was going to get to work. It was what Vera had assumed, but she felt relieved to see it happening. "He had almost a dozen sick visits in the first nine months. In that time Mary-Lee was also diagnosed with postpartum depression."

Betty refilled some coffee mugs and hummed her opinion. "A sick baby will make you feel all out of sorts."

Piper was the hammer about to hit the nail. "What does Mary-Lee say about all of this? She didn't testify on her own behalf."

"We don't know," Vera reported, fixing her eyes on Jay. "We haven't talked to her at all about it. Jay lost contact after her conviction."

"Wait," Michael put his coffee mug down and rubbed a hand over the streak of gray hair at his temple. "You don't know how she feels about the possibility of a new trial? The whole reason these trials get looked at in the first place is because the client is pushing for their own release. They are claiming their innocence or demanding a new trial. Mary-Lee may not want this."

Jay dropped his fork. "Are you suggesting my mother wants to spend the rest of her life in prison?"

"I'm suggesting we don't know if she's been in prison telling everyone she did this. We don't know if she wants to go through another trial or have this brought back into the public eye." Michael's frustration finally started to show again and like a well-trained tag team, Bobby jumped in.

"What you have to understand, Jay, is that people in prison already live with so many restrictions. It's important that they have a say in what happens to them whenever they can. I think everyone here will do what we can to help you, but not until we know it's what Mary-Lee wants."

Jay opened his mouth, looking like he might protest, but Betty interrupted. "You're asking the boy to stroll into prison and talk to his mom after not seeing her all these years? Then on top of that, he's supposed to tell her he's trying to get her out of there? Seems pretty heavy."

"Yeah," Jay agreed, giving Betty a little smile. "I wasn't planning on reaching out to her until I had something worth sharing."

Michael at least was kind enough to soften his expression before breaking the bad news. "We need to speak with her first. Non-negotiable. I'm sure it would feel better to walk in there with good news, but we have to know what she wants first. If you don't want to, that's all right. Bobby or I could go chat with her."

"If anyone is going to talk to her it's going to be me." Jay sighed. "I just have to figure out exactly what I'm going to say. It's been so long."

"I can go with you." Vera averted her eyes, not wanting him to have to turn her down face to face. She could understand if he wanted to do it alone, but it was important he knew he didn't have to.

"Yeah, maybe that would be good." He moved his mashed potatoes around with his fork and contemplated it. "Once I talk to her, if this is what she wants, then we all work together or something?"

"Damn skippy," Betty said, patting the counter. "You've got yourself a cop, a lawyer, a couple of moms and a grandma. I can't think of a better team to crack this."

Jules came up and put a hand on his shoulder. "And if it doesn't go the way you hope, I can't think of better group of people to help you get through it."

"Oh hell," Betty said, throwing her hands up. "Fine. You broke me. Have some pie. But no whipped cream. And I mean it."

CHAPTER 21

"Not quite what you imagined?" Michael grabbed his briefcase from the back seat and walked up to the visitor counter at the prison. Vera and Jay trailed nervously behind.

"I didn't expect it would take a week to get in to see her." Jay had been antsy waiting for their approval for visitation to go through. One key element of it was his mother accepting the request. Would she want to see him after all this time? Would she wonder what had taken him so long?

"We're here now. Remember what I told you. We have thirty minutes. You have to limit your physical contact. This was a long ride for us to get here, so while I would normally tell you to keep this a casual reintroduction, I think we should instead get right down to it."

"Once they have a chance to talk for a bit," Vera insisted. "They might want some time alone."

"No." Jay shook his head as Michael checked them all in. "No, it's better if you all stay. I want her to know why I'm here. I want her to understand it's about helping her get out. I don't want her thinking that it's only me wanting to see her."

Michael put a hand on his shoulder. "Even if that was the

case, that would be okay. She's still your mother. No circumstances will change that. Do what feels right in there. Vera and I will follow your lead."

Jay nodded but only to appease them. This wasn't personal. Not in the way they all thought. It wasn't about running back into the arms of the woman who brought him into the world. It was about justice. It was about knowing something your whole life and finally being able to prove it. It was about working his ass off to get into law school, even though it was way out of his league, and hanging on the edge of that cliff by his fingertips. All so he could bring himself to this moment and find people like this.

Any sense of hope evaporated at the sight of the uniformed guards with guns strapped to their waists. When the metal door slammed shut behind them and they were patted down, there was no sentimentalizing this. This was prison. This was where his mother had lived for decades.

The guard leading the way knocked on a door with a small glass window. The guard inside opened. "You've got thirty minutes. Knock on this door when you're ready."

"Are you ready?" Vera asked, but all Jay could muster was a grunt.

"Mrs. Stevens?" Michael asked as he put his briefcase on the table. "Thanks for seeing us today."

"Jeremy?" Her eyes locked in on him and scrutinized every tiny detail of his expression. "Hmm, you have that little scar on your forehead by your hairline from when you hit your head on the stone table."

Jay's hand went up to the spot, and he remembered the day it happened. More than that, he remembered the feel of his mother's arms around him as the doctor put in the stitches. "Sorry I haven't . . ."

"Don't apologize," she begged. "You have nothing to be sorry for in this. If anyone is innocent in this it's you." Vera and

Michael exchanged a brief worried look. Was she implying she was guilty?

Jay couldn't take his eyes off his mother. She had been a bronze-skinned, blonde beauty when he was young. Her smile beamed and her long mane of hair would sway back and forth as they'd walk through the fields near their house. He remembered falling a few steps behind, nearly lost in the tall wheat, when he'd catch a glimpse of her and instantly feel safe.

Today was different. Her skin was pale and her eyes were drawn and tired. The wrinkles around her mouth were deep, and she looked much older than his father, like she'd been weathered by the lack of life she'd had. Her once long blonde hair was gray and cropped close to her head. Where her strong arms once were, there were only twigs and skin.

"I could have reached out to you sooner," Jay apologized. "I wanted to. But then I thought it would be better to do something about this rather than just meet and know we couldn't do anything about the circumstances."

"Mrs. Stevens," Michael began.

"Please call me Mary-Lee."

"All right Mary-Lee. My name is Michael Cooper. I'm an attorney. This is Vera Pedro. She's my intern, as is your son Jay."

"You go by Jay?"

"Yeah, Dad thought it might be better with all the attention the case got. I took Grandma's maiden name too."

"Smart. Your dad was always very smart. How is he?"

"He's good. He remarried. Has some kids."

"Your siblings?"

"His kids." Jay took a seat across from her and Michael opted to stay standing. That left Vera to awkwardly join the conversation.

"I know it must feel intrusive with Michael and me here."

"We're in prison dear, it's sort of always intrusive. I'm glad to see Jay is with people, rather than alone."

"I'm not alone," Jay gulped. "You are. Why haven't you kept in contact with anyone? Daryl, Dad, me? You don't even reach out to your own lawyer."

"Freedom and captivity don't mix. There was no way I was raising you to come visit me in this place like that was normal. Everyone else, I wanted them to move on."

Michael drove home what he must have seen as the most important point. "I don't know too many people who are going to spend their life in prison and not reach out to their counsel at least occasionally. They want updates, appeals. You haven't pursued any of that. Why?"

"Jim Neerely was a nice man, but I'm almost certain he was a functioning idiot when it came to being a defense attorney. Daryl knew him from high school, and we didn't know what we were looking for in a lawyer. We only knew we couldn't afford to pay much. At the time I didn't think it mattered who defended me."

"Why is that?" Jay asked and then held his breath.

"I assumed this would all work itself out. I figured the misunderstanding that put me in prison could get sorted out."

"Because you didn't hurt Pauly." The words were undefined, not a statement and not quite a question.

"I didn't expect to be convicted," she replied, not answering the question the way he would have liked. "We were so young, and it all happened quickly."

Michael leaned against the cement block wall and rubbed his chin. "We don't have much time here today Mary-Lee, so please forgive my frankness. Jay would like to find an avenue to appeal your conviction. It's a long shot but I have some people who would be willing to help. We're here today to find out how you feel about that."

The question was obviously left vague for a reason. He didn't intend to lead her down one path or another.

"Jay, you're going to be a lawyer?"

"No," he laughed. "I won't make it through law school. It's a miracle I made it this far. I wanted to learn as much as I could about the legal system and make connections with people who could help."

"You did all that work for me?" Her eyes glistened with the hint of tears. "What a good man you are."

"Mary-Lee," Michael urged, "how would you feel if we worked on getting you an appeal?"

A loud siren blared as the lights in the room went dark.

"What's happening?" Vera cried as her fingernails plunged into Jay's forearm. There was a red strobe light that cast a glow in the room every few seconds. In that light, he could see the look of terror on her face. The look of sadness on his mother's.

"Stay calm," Michael said as he stepped back from the door. "It's some kind of lockdown I'm sure. The guard at our door is gone. We'll just stay put."

Over the intercom, dire-sounding orders and codes crackled to life. Voices barked out commands and screams could sometimes be heard in the background.

"Did they say fire?" Vera asked, now clinging to Jay in the dark. "Is something on fire?"

Mary-Lee seemed to be off in some distant place, hardly even blinking. "Mom, it's going to be all right."

"I know," she whispered. "It's just how things are here."

"So this is no big deal?" Vera asked, and Mary-Lee reached a hand out to comfort her.

"We just need to stay put," Michael said, leaning so he could see out the small glass window on the steel door.

"Are we locked in?"

"Technically. But that's a good thing."

Vera's voice was sharp. "It's not a good thing if there is a fire. Do you see smoke?"

"No smoke." Michael reported but leaned back quickly as two people ran by the door. "Jay move the table back and put it on its side. Get your mom and Vera behind it."

Jay didn't ask why. He didn't need to. It was clear something was happening. Something more than a drill or a minor disruption. Just as he got the table to its side a loud boom echoed down the hall.

"What was that?"

"A flash bang." Michael replied coolly. "It's a distraction device. That's all. Something must be going on in the common area down by the kitchen we passed. The guards will get it under control."

"There's been trouble brewing for a while," Mary-Lee reported as she crouched behind the table. "Once they realize we're still in here they're going to take me fast. The guards will want everyone accounted for quickly."

Another bang sounded and now smoke billowed down the hallway toward them.

"Can't someone come buzz the door and let us out?" Vera cried.

Jay pulled her in close. "I don't think we want to be out there right now. We're safe in here. That smoke won't get in through the steel door." Jay pulled his long sleeved button-down shirt off and tossed it over to Michael. He was only wearing an undershirt now and could feel Vera's shaking body clutching him. "Roll it up and put it at the bottom of the door."

The light continued to strobe. The siren still blared. And Jay could see his mother practically unaffected by the noise and chaos.

Michael crouched down as another shadow passed in front of the door. "We need to be quiet."

"Why?" Vera gasped. "Shouldn't we tell them we're in here so they can let us out? We should be doing something shouldn't we? Sitting here seems crazy."

Mary-Lee shook her head. "There is no better bargaining chip than a hostage. Plenty of people in here have nothing to lose. All they need to do is hit that button and buzz the door open. Then this whole thing changes. You're the kind of leverage anyone in here would want."

"So quiet," Michael said, leaning against the wall and staying crouched as low as he could.

"It'll be over soon," Jay whispered into Vera's hair as he held her. "We'll be out of here soon."

"I'm fine," Vera edged out, stiffening her back. "We're going to be fine." She said it as though she could will it to be true.

That was probably true for the three of them, but not for his mother. No matter what they found, no matter how hard they worked, the process would likely be slow and painful for her. There had been cases where DNA exonerated people and still they waited months, sometimes years for their release.

The flash of an impossible dream flew across his mind. What if in the commotion of whatever this was, Mary-Lee could walk straight out with them? She could get in the car, drive off, and get a fresh start.

The siren finally turned off. The lights flickered back to life.

"That's a good sign, right? We are going to be fine." Vera whispered. The shirt under the door hadn't kept all the smoke out, and Jay's eyes and throat stung. He could tell Vera and his mother were feeling the same.

"I see guards," Michael reported, looking thoroughly relieved. The door buzzed open a moment later and just as she suspected, they came quickly for Mary-Lee.

The guard pulled her up to her feet and restrained her with handcuffs. "I need you all to stay right where you are. You are in no imminent danger, but you have to be escorted out once we have someone available to do so.

"We didn't finish our conversation." Jay knew he sounded like a child who sat through his haircut but didn't get the lollypop.

"Sorry son," the guard grunted. He was covered in sweat and panting as he moved Mary-Lee toward the door.

"We are finished, Jay," his mother said through a forced smile. "You can see why you don't belong here. I won't drag you into my life. This isn't worth it."

"It's worth it to me."

"Don't come back here. I won't see you as visitors. It's okay to move on." She was gone a moment later, the door slammed shut, the buzzing sound telling them they were again locked in.

Jay stood with his mouth open, his chest torn to shreds. That was the only way to explain the pain. "No. No, that's not good enough."

"Jay, don't worry about it." Michael put a hand on his shoulder and spun him around. "She didn't say no. She just said don't come back here. We don't need to."

"You're still going to help?" Jay felt a wash of adrenaline leave his body. "Seriously?"

Michael leaned against the wall and continued looking out the small glass window of the door. "Have some faith, son. We move mountains."

CHAPTER 22

"Your father is going to kill me." Jay bit at his thumbnail.

He wasn't wrong. The second her father heard about what happened at the prison he'd be a nervous wreck. She considered downplaying it, but she knew the rumors around town would start flying. Not to mention her father would see it in her eyes.

"Michael already called him. I heard them talking." Jay let her go first as they walked into the auto shop.

"Try not to imagine how many things he could use in here to punish you." Vera cracked a small smile.

"So many tools."

"Have you two joined a prison gang?" Her father used a rag to wipe the oil off his hands and then tucked it into his pocket. "What the hell were you thinking? I have half a mind to tell Michael you aren't showing up to work tomorrow. You're an intern. You should be filling paper clip jars."

"It's part of the job, Daddy. You knew being a lawyer meant I'd be going into prisons, dealing with criminals."

"It's really my fault," Jay cut in. "This wasn't about Michael. It was more personal, and I shouldn't have asked Vera to come. It wasn't a good situation."

"I'd hope it isn't one you'd put her in again." Her father raised a brow and tipped his head. "I don't know exactly what you have going on in your life, but it won't negatively affect my daughter."

"Yes sir."

"Are you two finished?" Vera felt her blood racing. "I know the instinct is to sell me to a good family, Dad, in exchange for a goat and maybe a plot of land. However I don't intend to spend my days being jockeyed between men who feel like they know what is best for me. I'm going to be a lawyer. I'm going to be in tough situations. Was I scared today? Of course. That doesn't change anything. Life is going to be scary sometimes."

"I saw the story on the news," her father groaned. "They said it was a riot. If you would have been hurt, if something had happened to you, I don't know what I would have done."

Jay waved his hands. "I wouldn't have let anything ha—"

"All right, here we go again." Vera planted her hand on her hip. "Should I leave you two alone to plan my future? Maybe you can design a bubble I could walk around in. Today happened. It's over. We are moving on. Everything worked out today. I knew it would." She had said it over and over again as she sat crouched in that small room. There was no way to know she was right until it was all over, but still somehow she knew they'd get out of there. They had to. And they did.

Her father tucked his hands in the pockets of his overalls and lowered his voice. "I want you to take the summer off from this. Come work here like you always have. I need you here."

"Here where you can see me?"

"Here where you've always been. Your day in the courtroom will come. Before you know it, you'll be passing the bar and be off doing things I can't even imagine. But why does your summer have to be all this? I thought you'd be in Michael's office doing paperwork. Not these road trips. Not stirring up things from the past. Michael will understand. I can call him for you."

She moved in closer and kissed his cheek. "You're the best dad in the world. I love you. But I am not giving up my dream. This work is part of making that dream come true. It doesn't change anything between us."

"I've never been one to say under my roof, you'll live by my rules." He drew in a deep breath and seemed to choke on the next sentence. "But I think it's for your own good that you let this go for the summer."

"Are you saying if I don't come answer phones at the shop and give up an internship that could be a gateway to my future, you're kicking me out?" She stepped back, and her eyes went wide as saucers. "You aren't saying that because that has never been how things work with us."

"Things are changing."

Jay tried to step away but she caught his arm. "It's his mother in prison. Did you know that? That's who we were visiting today. Michael is going to help out with her case. I'm going to help. You've spent my whole life telling me about doing the right thing, protecting people I care about. Now here I am with a chance to do that, and you're telling me to quit or else. You don't mean that."

"If it is his mother, maybe that is more of a reason to get out of this. It'll be messy. I see the way he looks at you. This will go bad, and you'll get your heart broken or worse. Take it from a man who has lived through that kind of pain."

"You haven't lived at all." Vera was reeling. Never in all her years had her father given her an ultimatum. They were level-headed people. They talked things out; even when she was very young, he treated her with a level of respect. Now he'd crossed the line, and apparently she was going to do the same. "You haven't put yourself out there at all. Mom hurt you and you gave up. Locked yourself in this shop and pretended you had nothing else to offer to the world but oil changes and new brake pads. How many women have asked you out that you've turned down?

How many chances at happiness have you walked away from? I'm sorry I've been your whole life for so long and now I'm ready to go live mine. But you had to know this day would come."

"Vera," Jay pleaded as he tugged gently at her arm, "maybe you should go cool off a while."

"No." Vera turned on her heel and walked away. "I'm going to pack my bags."

CHAPTER 23

"Can you believe him?" Vera slammed the car door so hard Jay was worried the window might shatter. "He seriously pulled the *my house, my rules* bull? What has gotten into him?"

"Did you see the footage they were showing on the news about the prison riot? It was intense. He was obviously rattled. So were you by the way. I don't think we should act like it was no big deal." Jay drove without much direction. They could go back to Betty's and she would put them both up for the night, in very separate rooms. But that would likely come with more advice than either of them wanted at the moment.

"It was terrifying," she admitted. As glad as he was that the moment of fear was over, he still missed the chance to have her in his arms. She had cut him off earlier but it didn't change the facts. He'd have done anything to keep her safe. Anyone who'd wanted to get to her would have had to kill him first.

"Your dad will come around. He needs time to think this over. I'm sure tomorrow night you'll be sleeping in your own bed."

"Whose bed should I sleep in tonight?" She threw her hand up quickly. "Don't answer that. I didn't mean that the way it sounded. I can call a friend and crash there."

"Or . . ." Jay shrugged.

"Or what?"

"We could camp out under the stars tonight. Park the car somewhere. Open this sun roof and lay the seats back. It won't be comfortable but it might be fun. I could use the kind of quiet you can only get down here. Have you gotten used to the city at night yet?"

"No," she laughed. "It's all sirens and honking horns and people yelling. What the hell do people have to yell about all night?"

"Exactly. What is with the lights on all the time? You can't even see the stars. Why don't we grab some stuff from the store and hang out somewhere? You must know a good spot."

"And we'll just sleep?" She rolled her eyes. "Boys like you have been trying to get me to go parking with them for years. I never go."

"Men like me don't play games." He reached over and held her hand, pulling it to his lips and kissing it gently. "I could sit next to you all night and listen to you talk. I want know more about you."

"Like what?" She waved him off. "There isn't much to know. Edenville isn't exactly exciting, and I've lived here my whole life. I've been away at college but all I do is study."

"Then tell me about that. What's your study routine? You listen to music? Sit in one special chair at the library? I bet a girl like you has all sorts of superstitions."

"I don't rely on lucky charms to get my grades."

"Yeah, I don't recommend it. I've tried them all. And every gimmick. But mostly I study my ass off and barely pass. But it won't matter soon. Once we get traction on my mom's case, I won't need to go back to school. I can save myself a boatload of money and get my life back. I swear I'm going to toss out every law book I have."

"Pull up that way," she said, pointing to a small dirt road. "I used to read out there some nights when I couldn't get any work done at my house."

He pulled the car off the road and put it in park. She slid the sunroof open, and they both leaned their seats back. When Vera turned her head toward him, he couldn't help but do the same. She was better than looking at the stars.

"You've already worked so hard. Why not stick with it? I could tutor you." She winked playfully.

"It's not what I want to do with my life. It's an admirable field. You'll certainly do great at it. I just wanted to learn what I could to help my mother."

"What will you do for work?"

"I've done the math." He laughed. "I'll need eight full time jobs to be able to survive the debt. Should be easy."

"I'm serious. What do you plan to do?"

"I don't plan. Planning is not in my DNA. I remember my mother was very much the same way. Life was meant to be surprising, and she certainly made it that way."

"Then let me ask the question differently. If you could have any job you wanted, anything at all, what would it be?"

He tucked his hands behind his head and considered the question. "I'd probably teach. Maybe like second grade. I had a few teachers along the way who really helped me. I'm not sure I would have made it through without them looking out for me. I'd like to do that for someone else someday."

"I can definitely see you as a teacher. Sport coat with the patches on the elbows. Some goofy tie that makes the kids laugh. You'd even let them call you Mr. C."

"That is all very accurate."

"You know they're out looking for us right now. I'm sure Bobby has his patrol guys out with orders to take me home or something." She tucked her hair behind her ears and sighed.

"Let them come." He turned toward her and ran a thumb over her cheek. "We'll go on a high-speed chase right out of town. I'll drive all night if I have to."

"Where would you take me?" She leaned in, her wide smile getting closer by the second.

He thought of every place he'd never seen. Every corner of the earth he wanted to explore and how it would be made even better if she was with him. "I might not be able to do much on my teacher's salary."

"I'll be a high-powered attorney so I can take us around the world." Her lips were just a breath away from his.

"I don't mind being a kept man."

"Are you going to kiss me?" She hardly had the words out before his lips overtook hers. He knew the second this kiss ended everything in his life would be defined as either before or after it. Nothing would be the same. Not when a woman like Vera could overlook every one of his flaws.

Her hands reached out to his body, and though the car was not remotely accommodating, they couldn't seem to let go of each other. Not until she finally broke the kiss.

"Is this real?" Her eyes fluttered like she'd just woken from a dream. "I know the smartest thing for you to do right now is to get close to me. Michael and Bobby, they're going to help you out because they care about me and I seem to care about you. On paper, this is your best play."

Like a cannonball to the chest her words struck his heart with what felt like a fatal blow. "Vera, I'm not playing you. I can't believe you're even interested in being in this car tonight, let alone kissing me. You have this plan, this drive I can hardly imagine. I make as much sense in your life as an elephant in a little red wagon. I don't fit. I never will. Since the first minute we met, I've brought nothing but frustration and chaos to your life. I'm not playing a game. I'm lucky as hell."

"You are incredibly frustrating," she agreed. "And I'd have a much different experience if you weren't here right now. But I kind of feel like I'd be missing out on something great. Something I'd never be brave enough to do on my own. I wanted to make sure this was real."

"Vera," he leaned in and kissed her lips, lingering close to stare her straight in the eyes. "I'm a man of very few talents. I fail. I give up. I lose. For the first time, with you in my corner, I feel like losing is not an option. I've hung a lot on what happens this summer. Now you are one more thing I can't wait to happen. One more thing I'll do anything to have."

"You have me." She kissed him back. "You already have me."

CHAPTER 24

Rather than her alarm clock, it was the tap of a metal flashlight on a car window that woke her. The sun wasn't quite up yet, but it was coming fast. "Love birds, you two better fly on home."

It was a young officer she recognized from high school. He'd been a year or two ahead of her. Sean Christy. He had the same goofy look as always, and his teeth were slightly too big for his mouth. He reminded her of a sweet golden retriever who occasionally got caught in the loop of chasing his own tail. The nicknames in school were relentless, and he likely took pleasure in paying back his bullies with speeding tickets. But Vera had always been kind to him. Hopefully that might pay off.

Vera shot up to a sitting position and wiped at her eyes as he rolled down the window. "We're not doing anything. We were just sleeping."

Jay groaned. "We're going."

"Sean, please don't tell my father you found us here. Please."

Sean laughed. "You sound like the juniors in high school I caught up here last week. You're a grown woman, Vera; you can drive around with whoever you want. But this here is private property, and you have to move along."

"I know I'm a grown woman," she shot back curtly. "I'm just not looking for a town scandal. You know how everyone can be around here."

"I didn't call the car in. Just hit the road, and no one will know. I think you two are working on your own scandal. I heard about the case Michael is taking on. It's your mother?"

"Yeah." Jay was still half asleep as he tried to roll the ache out of his neck. Sleeping in the car hadn't been the smartest idea.

"You know my uncle lived in California, and he almost went to prison when his daughter died. They said he shook her. He worked out in the fields all day and they said he came home one night tired and frustrated. The baby was crying like crazy. His wife was sick and sleeping at her mother's house to try to recover. He put the baby in the crib to cry it out and fell asleep. A couple hours later he woke up and she was dead. Cold."

"I'm sorry to hear that," Vera said, not sure Jay was up for such a graphic story, considering his own circumstances.

"But he didn't shake her." Sean put his flashlight away and continued his story. "He gets arrested, some expert says the results show he did. They testify and he's convicted. But two years later some other expert comes out and says the first expert is incompetent. That first guy didn't run all the appropriate tests. He heard the circumstances and drew a conclusion. The MRI supported his conclusion and a jury thought that was enough."

"So what happened?" Jay asked, now sounding fully awake and interested.

"It was meningitis. The scans can look similar in some instances. They ran tests on the samples they had and confirmed it. They let my uncle go. He has never been the same, but at least it cleared his name. I thought maybe that would help. The experts, they aren't always right."

"Yeah," Jay agreed, and Vera saw the spark of hope returning to his eyes. "They rely on these people to say what happened, and the jury will believe anything they say."

"But Pauly wasn't shaken, and he was tested for many kinds of illnesses." Vera thought back to the expert testimony she read. "The doctor concluded the blood work showed Pauly had been poisoned."

"Are there more samples?" Jay sat up a little straighter. "We could have tests performed."

"What lab would we do that in?" Vera challenged. "What would we have them tested for? It's a great story, Sean, one that turned out favorably, but it's a long shot in Mary-Lee's case." She was talking more to Jay than Sean now.

"Oh yeah," Sean said, backing up a few steps as the engine roared to life. "I just thought I should let you know."

"Thanks, dude," Jay said as he pulled out, kicking up gravel as he went.

"They did the tests on Pauly," Vera said as she buckled her seat belt. "We know the blood work showed high levels of glycol. The ingredient in antifreeze. The coroner confirmed that in the autopsy. He was one of the leading specialists in the south and was brought in specifically for Pauly's case."

"And Sean's uncle sat in prison for two years thinking the same thing. The specialists can be wrong. Where was the autopsy done? Where would the samples be?"

"They may have been destroyed by now. It's not an open case. So many years have passed. I know you're looking for some magic bullet, but that's very unlikely."

"I spent last night kissing you. You'll have to forgive me, but I'm starting to believe in the impossible."

CHAPTER 25

"Why are you dropping me off?" Vera had an uneasy feeling. They'd grabbed all the files and found the lab that did the testing for Pauly. It was three hours south and still operational. Their phone call to find out how long samples were stored proved successful. All samples were stored indefinitely. The lab had ample storage on site and until someone requested something be destroyed it stayed intact.

"You should talk to your dad. I can go to the lab." He had a fierce kind of look in his eyes that unsettled her.

"You need some kind of court order or a hell of a lot of money to get them to run the tests again. Or to broaden the types of test they're willing to do. You can't smooth talk your way through this."

"I've got it. Make up with your dad. That's important right now. I'll call you later tonight." He pulled up in front of her house and put the car in park. He wasn't getting out. He wasn't walking her to the door. There would be no kiss goodbye. Something was forming. A storm on the horizon. A danger that made the hair on her arms stand up.

"What are you planning?" She didn't make a move to get out.

"Are you going to break in? Steal the samples? They'd become completely useless in court if you did that."

"I know that."

"So, you'll force them somehow. Hostages maybe? This is ridiculous. Your mother didn't want you to visit her in prison. She doesn't want you trading your freedom for hers. Slow down. Take a breath. We'll figure something else out. Maybe Michael has a favor he could call in."

"I'm done waiting, Vera. Daryl might be hiding something, but he didn't have the opportunity to hurt Pauly as frequently as he was sick. There were so few other people in the baby's life. If it wasn't my mother, this has to be the answer. There has to be something they could test for that would prove he wasn't poisoned."

"Then we will find a reason to request retesting."

"Are we playing pretend?" Jay looked at roof of the car. "You know how long the backlog is in these labs. DNA testing for cases can sit around for years after a request at testing is made. Years."

The gravity in the truth yanked her back to earth and slammed her down. He was right. But it didn't mean he should storm into a lab brandishing God knows what and forcing them to retest samples. They didn't even know what they should test for.

"Then we'll find money to pay to have the testing done privately."

"A bake sale maybe?" He wasn't wavering because she wasn't giving him a remotely reasonable option.

"Then we do what Sean said." She reached out and took his hand in hers. "We look into the expert who testified at the trial. Maybe there are things he overlooked, and we utilize that information to make an appeal, and with the appeal, Michael helps write a petition to expedite the testing. That could work. But we'd have to figure out what to test for. And we'd have to undermine the credibility of a well-respected professional. It's still a better option than anything you're considering."

"Better but not faster. Not to mention this doctor has probably worked hundreds of cases over the years. How would we even know where to start?"

"You have a super genius at your disposal." She pointed to herself and smiled. "I can turn the man's whole career into a spreadsheet in an hour. If there is anything to find, we'll find it."

"I'm not sure you've given me a good enough reason to use your plan instead of mine."

She cut his words off with a kiss. Vera crossed over the center console, and sat on his lap, locked her arms around his neck, and cut his words off with a kiss. "You don't get to throw your life away. It's too mixed up with mine now."

CHAPTER 26

Betty had been kind enough to lend them the restaurant after closing. Vera set up a presentation with a projector and handed out stacks of documents to everyone. The crowd was made up of very different skill sets. Bobby was the cop. Piper was the social worker. Jules was a mom and a whip-smart, no-bull woman. Betty and her husband, Clay, were always quick with sage and relevant advice. Dr. Toms, a friend of Betty who worked at the local hospital, was willing to give general opinions. Michael brought his obvious expertise. Even Vera's dad was there, but he joked it was only for Betty's pot roast.

Five of them had laptops open and note pads; the others had plates waiting for more food.

"Thanks for coming. We wanted to get lots of eyes on this and get everyone's ideas. Here is what we know.

"Pauly Stevens died at nine months old. He was chronically ill and saw only his pediatrician. He was never referred to a specialist and no testing was done while he was alive to determine what might have caused his symptoms. The doctor in the emergency room, suspecting poisoning, ran blood work which came back positive for high levels of glycol along with some other abnormal chemical compounds. He alerted the police and child protective services. Mary-Lee and Daryl were kept away from Pauly, and he seemed to be recovering some. Then at the urging of child services, who felt the baby should have supervised time with his mother, Mary-Lee was allowed back in for a visit. Twenty-four hours later Pauly died of some kind of cardiac event they concluded came from a lethal dose of poison."

Most of the facts and a timeline were projected on the makeshift screen of the empty restaurant wall. Betty had reluctantly approved taking down her knick-knacks for one night.

Jay held his breath as he watched everyone scan the information. It was Dr. Toms, with his wild gray hair and crooked tie, who spoke up first. "If Mary-Lee had contact with the child twenty-four hours before his death it would be highly unlikely that she, under supervision, would have been able to give him a dose of antifreeze. Even if he had the symptoms, it would have been apparent right away. Judging from his chart, he was not exhibiting any symptoms until fifteen hours after her visit. I can't think of any poison that would increase glycol levels to a fatal amount but wouldn't start until fifteen hours later."

Vera jotted the note down frantically. "The ER doctor who first read the blood results testified he had never seen results like this before. He had only independently read lab results six times before that night as he was new on the job. Does that seem worrisome?"

Dr. Toms looked at the page Vera handed over. "The results are fairly straightforward. He was correct that the glycol level was high. But he didn't do any further testing. At this stage of the treatment he hardly had a full view of the child's medical history. I would say at a minimum he was acting rashly."

"Would you say negligently?" Michael asked.

"I wouldn't be able to say that." Dr. Toms read on. "If this child came through the ER today and the parents seemed otherwise engaged and cooperative, while I would ensure they were supervised, I would not separate them completely. It can be quite a shock to a small child to be pulled from his mother's arms and poked and prodded by strangers. I would also do some further testing beyond the one blood test."

Betty hummed and nodded. "I don't know any of the jargon on these medical papers or anything, but I will say it's strange that a baby was sick so many times and never went to see a specialist."

Dr. Toms agreed. "Yes, the pediatrician's notes kept dismissing the illness as colic and then stomach bugs. It could certainly have been an allergy since it seemed to get more frequent once solid foods were introduced."

"Here are the coroner's findings," Vera said as she handed them out. "I've also summarized the other four hundred sixty-two cases he consulted on over the years. There are nineteen child deaths. I ruled out the six that were due to physical accidents. Of the thirteen that remained he deemed eleven to be homicide."

Piper flipped quickly through the papers and then scanned the notes Vera switched to on the projector. "That seems high. Were any others poisonings?"

"Three." Vera couldn't hide the note of alarm in her voice. "Three of his other eleven cases were marked as death by intentional poisoning."

Dr. Toms jumped in. "Let's remember he's considered in expert in the field. It's likely just as in Mary-Lee's case, he was called in because of concern for what was already identified. It's not as though random cases came to him."

"True." Michael took a cookie off the tray Betty was passing around.

"Chocolate chip or raisin?" Vera's father asked.

"Really, Dad, that's your question right now?" She rolled her eyes.

"I have been fooled before by dried fruit pretending to be chocolate. I try not to make the same mistake twice."

"Chocolate of course," Betty said proudly. "Take two."

"I wasn't exactly expecting snacks at this presentation." Vera's hand rose to her hip and rested there, showing her annoyance. To Jay it was cute. Like a kid selling lemonade and demanding her quarter.

Bobby grabbed a handful of cookies and Betty gave him a look, forcing him to put one back. "You planned a meeting at Betty's restaurant, with Betty, and you didn't think there would refreshments? I'm assuming the cookies are the appetizer. She'll probably pull a turkey out of the oven in half an hour."

Betty took back one more cookie from him. "You're the only turkey in this room, Bobby."

"Then why did I hear the oven timer go off?" Bobby asked.

Clay answered with a chuckle. "Because my wife thought we might all want to take some food home for lunch tomorrow. It's lasagna, not a turkey."

"Can we get back to this?" Vera asked, looking to Jay for support, but he was too busy pouring milk to go with his cookies.

Piper was her only ally. "Go on, Vera, what else do you have?"

"Dr. Toms, I was hoping you might be able to tell us if there is anything that stands out on the coroner's report."

"He does note there were crystalline structures in the patient's brain. That's also an indication of antifreeze poisoning."

"What other testing did he do?"

"As far as I can see this was a standard autopsy with no additional testing performed. He relied on the initial blood screen done at the hospital, along with the statements and medical records leading up to the death. Then he drew the conclusion that seems most obvious."

Jay put his glass down and started pacing the room. "How can you default to the most obvious answer and still be considered an expert?"

Vera's father, with a mouthful of cookies, answered first. "Occam's razor."

"What?" Vera asked with the look only a daughter can give her father when he's embarrassing her.

"Occam's razor," he repeated more clearly, swallowing the cookie. "It's a problem-solving principal that says the most obvious answer is usually the right answer. This doctor played the odds. Mechanics do it all the time. You can't know for sure what might be wrong, but the option for repairs that has the least amount of challenges and the highest likelihood to be right is where you start."

"I know what Occam's razor is, Dad, I'm just wondering how you do."

"You leave a million flash cards around the house. I found that one in the couch last year." He took another big bite of his cookie and shrugged.

"Wait . . . this is odd." Dr. Toms keyed a few things into his laptop. "There's a handwritten note in the margin of his report. It says '*DDA?*' But then it's crossed out."

"What does DDA mean?" Michael leaned over the doctor's shoulder and looked for himself.

"It's a genetic disorder. It's quite rare, and to be honest it doesn't really fit the symptoms fully. But there's an infant screening for DDA. If Pauly had tested positive for it, it would have been in his medical records."

Jules snatched Michael's laptop. "Not necessarily. They only made that a mandatory newborn screening eighteen years ago. Prior to that not all states included it. South Carolina didn't."

Jay gave Vera a desperate look. He'd felt sturdy most of his life. Self-sufficient. Like a building built on a solid foundation. But now, so close to the things he wanted most, he felt paper-thin.

A flower growing through the cement of the sidewalk with a million tourists passing over. "Could that be it? Maybe he was already sick?"

Dr. Toms shook his head. "It really doesn't match the symptoms close enough. DDA presents much younger. The life expectancy if undiagnosed and untreated is usually a month at most. Pauly was nine months old."

Jay's voice was urgent but not nearly as burning as the feelings swirling in him. He masked that, not wanting to be accused of being too emotional to be objective. "Then why write it in the column of the report? It has to mean something."

Michael held up a hand. "Did he test for it?"

"No, not that I can see."

"Then that might be something." Michael jotted a few notes down. "If he considered it and didn't test for it, we might be able to make a case that he was negligent in his assessment."

"He probably came to the same conclusion I did," Dr. Toms argued. "It's highly unlikely DDA was the cause."

"We know that, but a judge might not." Michael looked to Vera and that's when Jay knew how smart she really was. A second source in the room.

"Yes," she said, snapping her fingers. "We could have her lawyer petition the court with the original copy of this document. It's been done before. Let me think. Morris v. Something."

"Ricklens!" Michael shouted, turning his laptop back in his direction. "Yes, it was a note in the corner of a legal brief. The lawyer jotted down something in the margin about a witness. He later said the individual had never been brought to his attention. When the document surfaced, he was bagged. It was enough to get a new trial."

"We can site that case in the petition. I can start writing it tonight."

"Look at my girl." Her father beamed. "She can start writing it tonight."

"This doesn't feel like enough," Jay admitted. "If he didn't have DDA, we still don't know what happened."

Dr. Toms looked at him empathetically. Like a person about to cancel plans. "It's unlikely even with all the information you have here, we'd be able to find the cause of death if it wasn't poisoning."

"What would you do, Dr. Toms? Surely there could be more." Betty didn't seem to take no as an answer. There had to be more that could be done, and Jay was grateful for that ferocity right now.

"I'd find someone involved in biochemistry and molecular biology. Then I'd see if they could help isolate conditions that mimic this type of poisoning. If there are viable tissue samples still remaining, I'd get those tested. If this was some kind of underlying disease, it would be rare."

"And I, as his sibling, would have it too? Which I don't." Jay sighed.

"No not really. Many genetic diseases and abnormalities are caused by the combination of genes from both parents. Since you only share a mother, it would be unlikely that you would have the same condition. Or any other children Pauly's father had with a different woman."

Piper chimed in, "But could the parents, Mary-Lee and Daryl, both be tested to see if they are carriers of the condition?"

"It really depends on the condition." Dr. Toms shrugged. "This is way outside my area of expertise. I triage and do emergency medicine. This is a different type of science. You need someone who has studied it for a long time."

Bobby fixed his eyes on Jay. "And we might be chasing ghosts anyway. This case might not be easy to swallow, but it doesn't mean the jury was wrong."

"I know that." Jay could still see reality. He didn't like it. It was intrusive and unpalatable. But he hadn't completely shoved it aside. "I know there is a chance my mother was so alone, so tired, and so sad that she poured antifreeze into her child's bottle. Or mixed it into his cereal. But there is a chance she didn't. There's a chance she loved him and lost him and then sat in a cage all these years face to face with her grief. Everyone I talked to said they lost touch with her. Everyone. No one deserves to be that kind of lonely."

Betty came up and handed Jay another cookie. "You can be her son and not get her out of prison. You can be in her life and not fix everything. If you think you have to choose, you are wrong."

"I know I don't have to choose. But I do have to try."

CHAPTER 27

Vera knew the library was closing. She heard the announcements, and she saw the librarian turning off the lights. But the breakthrough hadn't come. The moment of euphoria she usually experienced when researching something and coming to the right conclusion was out of her reach.

She closed the book she was scouring over and stuffed it in her bag. She was a lawyer not a doctor. Finding a medical condition that could appear like a poisoning seemed simple at first, but she was striking out.

Always vigilant as her father taught her, she grabbed the car keys and tucked her phone away, not wanting to be distracted as she crossed the parking lot outside the library. It was later than she thought, and the lot was nearly empty. Out of habit she put her keys between her fingers like a weapon, ready to gouge an eye if she had to. Who knew if it would really work? That was what they always told women to do in self-defense classes.

But as usual, the second she got in the car her father let her use and locked the door, she felt silly. This was Edenville. Bad things rarely happened in a town so sleepy.

"If you scream, this knife goes into the base of your neck."

The voice was unfamiliar and chilling. Like the sound of steel on steel. The words slicing through the silence.

"What?" She made a move to turn around, but the person punched the seat.

"Shut up and drive."

Her mind sprinted through every piece of advice and every statistic she'd heard about abductions. She landed on just one. Secondary locations. The odds of survival once you left the abduction scene were diminished. If you gave up control of the current surroundings you gave up your best shot at living.

She dropped the keys to the ground and fumbled as she cried. "Wait. The keys."

"Hurry up!" He punched the seat again. "You're going to be sorry you ever met him. You're going to be sorry you stuck your nose where it didn't belong."

She bent to get the keys from the floor of the car, out of his immediate reach. Grabbing at the handle she swung the door open and lunged out. Low enough to get away.

The man cursed, and she clicked the lock button before he could get his door open. It wouldn't hold him for long but all she had to do was get back in the library. There were enough employees there to keep him from doing something stupid. Or at least she prayed it would deter him.

"Help! Help!" she screamed until her voice cracked. Until her words felt like needles in her throat. "Help me!"

The janitor at the library stumbled out, looking concerned, holding his mop like weapon.

Vera was brave enough for a moment to turn back to her car. The man was wearing a mask, brandishing a knife, and clearly still considering charging at her.

"Get inside," the janitor ordered as he yanked her arm and slammed the door shut. "Jilly, call the police. Is the side door still unlocked?"

DEFENDING INNOCENCE

"No, I locked it." The librarian lunged for the phone, her eyes wild with worry. "What's happening?"

"There's a man in my car. He has a knife."

"Oh my gosh, Vera. Are you hurt?"

"Just get the police here," the janitor ordered, ushering Vera behind the counter where the librarian was. "You two crouch down."

The adrenaline was coursing through her body like a racecar leading the pack. The blood in her ears was percussive, thudding to the beat of her racing heart. The library had been her haven. It was a quiet place where she could think and explore the pages of brilliance that lined every wall. Now all she could hear was her breathing and the panicked explanation to the person on the other end of the line as the librarian gasped out answers to their questions. It felt like an eternity before the sound of sirens broke the silence.

Whoever that was couldn't get her now. Not with the police in the parking lot. She should have been flooded with relief. Instead there was only dread. A replaying of his words. Words that were vague but a message that couldn't be misinterpreted. This was about Jay. This was about Mary-Lee.

"Vera?" The knock on the door sounded thunderous in the echoing halls of the empty library. "It's Bobby."

The janitor looked through the side window and unlocked the door. "She's right back there. I saw the man. He had a big hunting knife."

"Vera?" Bobby called again.

Her knees quivered as she stood and instantly burst into tears. Through the blurry haze she could see Bobby breathe a sigh of relief. He was certainly considering what it would have been like to have to wake her father and tell him horrible news.

Another officer was through the door a moment later, and Bobby put him right to work. "Take this man's statement. He saw the subject. I want the description out over the radio in the next five minutes. Wake people up. Get the dogs out here. I want this guy caught."

"Yes, sir."

"Tell me what happened," Bobby said, shepherding her toward a table where she could sit.

"I don't know. I got in the car, and this guy was in the back seat. I usually check the back seat. I didn't tonight. I would never just get in like that."

"It's all right. Take a breath and tell me what he said. What did he want?"

"He wanted me to drive. But I wouldn't. I read if you go to a secondary location, statistically it's bad."

"You're right." He put his hand on her shoulder and smiled. "Very smart."

"He said he would stab me in the neck if I moved. I pretended to drop my keys, and when I bent down I jumped out of the car and ran. I screamed my head off."

"Good, that's good. Exactly what you should have done. Did he say anything else?"

"Yes." She wiped at her eyes. "He said I never should have stuck my nose in this, and I'm going to wish I never met him, meaning Jay. He had to mean Jay, right? And the case. He was talking about the case. Right? What else could it be?"

"We don't know that for sure." Bobby grabbed the radio off his shoulder and called out a code she couldn't decipher. "I want you to stay put. I'm going to talk to the officers who are arriving. I need to tell them what we know and what to do next."

"Who would want us to stop? Who would care so much about the outcome of this case that they would kill me?" Vera's words spilled out like a waterfall.

"He was probably trying to scare you, to threaten you so you'd back off. We can't know why but if we catch him I promise you, I'll find out." Bobby had a look in his eye she felt compelled to believe. An assertion that she felt had to be true. He meant what he was saying, and in that she found the slightest bit of comfort.

She sat and could feel the hard seat beneath her and smell the welcoming aroma of old books that had always made her feel at home. That was what was grounding her to the moment. Otherwise she would have been swept right back to the sound of the man in her backseat. The shine of the blade in his hand as he crossed the parking lot.

"My dad," she muttered mindlessly. "He's going to find out and he's going to try to get here."

She tugged on the sleeve of the closest officer. "You all right?" he asked.

"My father. You have to call my dad. He's going to try to get here."

"We have everything shut down," the officer reported. "He'll have to stay where he is."

"No you don't understand." She let out a breathy laugh just as the officer's radio crackled with some report. A man. Her father. Fighting his way through the closed road.

"Let him through."

It was a few moments later when an officer escorted her dad into the dimly lit library.

"What happened?" he gasped with tears in his eyes. "Who did this?"

"I don't know," she cried, crumpling into her father's arms. There was no difference between this moment and the time she broke her arm roller skating. He felt just the same. She was bigger. The pain was different. But what she craved was the same.

"You're all right," her father promised. "It's all right now."

There was no logic to his assertion. No proof of what he was saying. Yet she let herself believe him.

CHAPTER 28

"They got him," Betty reported as she pumped her fist in victory. "You can't run in Edenville. We'll shut it down and corner you like the rat that you are."

Jay still didn't feel any better. Knowing the man who held Vera hostage was captured should have given him some peace. It didn't. There was only rage in him. Rage and an occasional burst of helplessness.

"How about tea?" Betty filled the kettle before he could answer. Jay didn't like tea. It was always bitter to him but he knew a steaming mug would be in front of him soon no matter what.

"Tell me again what happened." He closed his eyes and conjured up the image as Betty had first described it.

"You may be a glutton for punishment but that doesn't mean I have to inflict it. I told you they caught the man. She is safe and with her father. There is no point in going over it again." The tea kettle clanked onto the stove and she grabbed two mugs.

"Edenville doesn't have a lot of random crime does it? How often do people hide in the back of a car with a knife around these parts?"

"Bobby will find out what's going on." Betty grabbed her phone and pressed it between her shoulder and her ear, its long spiral cord stretching between her and the phone's base on the wall. "You better tell me something before this boy runs out of here wielding a butter knife." She looked at Jay and rolled her eyes. There were humming noises and nods of understanding. Then she placed the phone back on the wall.

"You have a direct line to the police station?" Jay wouldn't be surprised if the answer was yes.

"I know Bobby will pick up when I call. Apparently the crime wasn't so random. He's going to come by and talk with you soon. There was a threat. It might be related to your mother's case."

"Daryl." Jay pounded a fist to the table. "I knew he was being way too accommodating. He was hiding something, and he's willing to hurt people to keep that safe. He must be the one who hurt Pauly.

"You might need a pogo stick to make those kinds of leaps. We don't know anything yet." She sliced a few lemons and sprinkled some sugar into the mugs.

"You think Vera has a lot of enemies? A girl like her doesn't exactly go around pissing people off. If anything I don't know how you could be around Vera and not like her."

"I agree."

Jay dropped his head into his hands. "Are you sure she's all right?" Images flashed through his mind. How close was the knife to her? Did he put his hands on her at all? Rage simmered in his stomach like rice burning to the bottom of a pan.

"Bobby wouldn't lie to me. He knows better. She's upset but unharmed. They're getting to the bottom of it. I think you have to focus on what's important."

"You say that as though there is only one thing. Like I'm supposed to know what's important."

The kettle whistled and Betty tended to it without hesitation.

"You already know. You may not want to face it but you know. There is this case, your mother, it's been weighing on you your whole life. A shadow attached to your heels chasing you around. The odds that it's going to change in the near future are slimmer than a hungry stray cat."

"Vera?"

"Oh lordy child, can you please stop with the nonsense. The way you're feeling right now, the pit in your stomach. Listen to it. That part of you that's wondering what it would be like to lose her. The answer to that question. That's what important right now."

"Are you expecting me to forget about my mother? You think those have to be mutually exclusive causes?"

"They might be. You might have to choose one." Betty slid a mug of tea to him. "And as hard as you might want to fight it, only one of those two options will give you the peace you're looking for. Fighting for your mother might push Vera away. But pulling Vera closer might someday make you two strong enough to actually help your mother. As a mother myself I can tell you I want my children to live their lives. The future is what matters."

"My mother should have a future too. If this guy is out to get me or Vera, then that tells me there is more to the story. It means someone wants to stop us. If my mother was guilty no one would care."

"Drink your tea." Betty patted his hand. "Hold on to that feeling. When it's this scary to think about someone you care about getting hurt, it's a message."

"Trust me. I'm getting it loud and clear."

CHAPTER 29

They'd given her the choice, and it was easy to decide. The last place she wanted to be was the police station. They offered to bring her home and ask all the questions they needed to in the comfort of her own living room. What she hadn't expected was the crowd. Michael was sitting on the steps and half the neighbors were starting to gather around.

"You good?" Michael met her eyes but then looked past to judge Bobby's nonverbal assessment.

"They caught him," Bobby said stoically as they walked into her living room. "I've got my best detective on it now. It sounds like he's going to crack and tell us who sent him. Once we have that I'll get my other officers working on it. I don't think this was random."

Her father huffed and folded his arms across his chest. "We don't need to do this tonight do we? She needs to get some sleep."

"I'll stay in the area and keep an eye on the house tonight." Bobby walked around the living room taking a quick look around. "You've got my number. Just call me if you need anything."

Vera shook her head and touched her father's shoulder gently. "I want to hear if there are any updates. I know this is about the case. Who would send someone here to threaten me? There has to be a reason why."

"Who cares?" her father shouted. "It doesn't matter. Whatever it is, it isn't happening again. None of it is your problem. You got caught up in something and it nearly cost you your life."

"We don't know the details yet," Michael said, trying to calm him down. "Bobby's team is on it. When we know more we can make a plan."

There was a pulse of a thought throbbing at her temple. She wanted Jay. No one knew the case as well as he did. No one would be as passionate about finding the answers as Jay. And if she were being honest, no one would make her feel as safe.

"How is Jay?" She fidgeted, tucking her hair behind her ears. "Does he know?"

Bobby grabbed his ringing cell phone, but answered her first. "He knows. He's with Betty." He stepped away and Vera tried hard to hear as much of his phone conversation as possible.

"Damn." Michael cracked his knuckles. He was a few steps closer and clearly picking up the thread of it.

"What?" Vera felt the hair on the back of her neck stand up. "What did you find out?"

Bobby tucked his phone away and grimaced. "It's still an ongoing investigation."

"But? You know something." Her father's nerves were rubbed raw.

"The assailant was Greggory Lindley. He's got a good sized rap sheet full of breaking and entering. Mostly petty stuff. Under the pressure of more significant charges he cracked pretty easily. According to his statement Daryl Stevens hired him to come to town and threaten you."

"Daryl?" Vera's voice shook. "Pauly's father. He was so helpful. So positive. He said he wanted Mary-Lee free. That he would do anything he could to help. Why would he send someone here to try to get us to stop?"

Bobby gave Michael a knowing look. "We're still gathering information. Greggory didn't have an answer to why, just a bank wire and instructions from Daryl. He's going to be facing a lot of charges. I'm sure he'll be willing to talk to with the right motivation."

"Who cares why," her father boomed. "This man could have killed my daughter tonight. He hid in the back seat of her car and could have stabbed her. You're trying to figure out why this man did it?"

"Daddy, please, you have to understand this is bigger than just me and what happened tonight."

"My world is never bigger than you." He turned toward Michael and Bobby. "I know you both have daughters. You both can put yourself in my shoes. I want the man who ordered this to pay for what he's done."

Michael nodded his agreement. "I understand. I'm sorry Vera was the target of this idiot. We're going to get to the bottom of it."

"Let's go to bed please, Vera." Her father reached out his hand and waited for her to take it.

"I want to see Jay." It felt like a betrayal. Something selfish and weaponized. "I need to talk to him tonight. He and I can figure out what Daryl is hiding. I know we can."

A band of fathers made an unspoken agreement, Bobby finally vocalizing it. "There's nothing to do tonight, Vera. You've been through something traumatic. At some point the adrenaline will wear off. The emotions will get bigger and harder to wrestle. The best thing you can do is sleep. I'll check in with you tomorrow morning."

"Fine." She could tell by their crossed arms and their furrowed brows she'd be no match for the paternal brick wall they'd built. "If you're looking for me in the morning I'll be in the office with Michael."

"Take the day off," Michael insisted. "Bobby's right. This stuff can sneak up on you. One minute you think you're fine the next minute you're back in that car feeling like he's right behind you."

"I'm not letting this one guy—"

Bobby cut her off. "We don't know if he was working alone. That's the point Vera. It's not clear how desperate Daryl is or what his motive might be. There could be someone else in town trying to hurt you. I need you to lay low and let us protect you. There will be an officer outside your house for as long as it's needed. Local units are arresting Daryl tonight. I'm going to loop in the detectives. We're going to get to the bottom of this."

"Thank you, Bobby." Her father shook their hands and showed them out. "I feel better knowing you're on the job."

Vera looked around the room. At least the three of them felt better. She certainly didn't. Maybe they were right. Maybe the walls would come crashing in on her the second this adrenaline wore off. But right now, all she wanted was to sit in a room with Jay and dig through details and find the answer that had been eluding them.

"I'm going to bed," she lied. "Thanks for the help today."

She grabbed her bag and shuffled slowly to her room as Bobby and Michael saw themselves out. Her hand was on her cell phone before she even closed her bedroom door. She knew he'd pick up.

CHAPTER 30

"I'm so sorry," Jay sputtered out when he answered the phone. "Vera I never would have brought you in to something that could be so dangerous. I had no idea Daryl would be capable of something like this."

"I'm all right, Jay. This wasn't your fault. We had no idea Daryl would try to sabotage the case. We need to find out why."

"I know." He felt his arms tingle with relief. Hearing her voice was like the rock of a hammock on a summer day. "I'm going to find something."

She let out a breathy laugh and he wished he was holding her instead of the phone. "Are you going to use your wit and intellect to piece it all together?"

Jay smiled. Even after the night she had there was still time to tease him. "Vera I can't ask you do anything else. Not after tonight. The thought of…" he trailed off not wanting to make her relive the details.

"Daryl couldn't have killed Pauly." Her assertion seemed out of place. How was she already moving past the fear? "He didn't have the opportunity on any other occasion besides the event that put Pauly in the hospital. There was no record of him visiting the baby. I don't think that's what this is about. You were right the first time. He's hiding something. That's what we need to figure out."

Jay closed his eyes and dropped down on to the bed. Betty's footsteps had quieted half an hour ago, and he didn't want to wake her or Clay up. "They're arresting him tonight. Bobby will make sure the police down there get an answer out of him. That's not what we should be thinking about."

"What should we think about?" Her voice was quiet and childlike. "Isn't this why you're here?"

"It's why I came." He thought of her sweet smile. "I don't think it's why I'm still here. When we got the call tonight, there was a little while before I knew you were all right."

"Well, I was."

"Betty gave me some good advice."

"That isn't a very exclusive club you've joined."

"I don't think I can have both. Trying to help my mother has consumed me for years. I've always imagined my life, the part that mattered, would start after I got some sort of resolution. I've made sure of it. I just keep pushing off the idea of something more."

"Can't you have both?" Vera sounded hopeful but still guarded.

"Doesn't tonight answer that question? I'm risking one for the other."

"I would never ask you to give up the fight for your mother's freedom for me. Especially now that we know Daryl has something to gain by keeping us quiet. You should come over now and we could work."

"If I could get my hands on you right now, work would be the farthest thing in my mind. Vera, I just want to hold you and know you're all right."

"Then come."

"How many officers are stationed at your house?" He laughed at the image that popped in his head. If the people of Edenville who loved Vera had their way there would be tanks parked in her driveway.

"Just Bobby for tonight."

"You think I can get by him? Maybe throw stones at your window again? Not a great idea tonight."

"Then we're stuck. I wanted fall asleep with you." He could practically see her pouting now.

"Then sleep. I'll stay on the phone. I can even play some of my cheesy music in the background if that helps."

"It might." She yawned and he could hear her blankets rustling around.

"I can't come hold you tonight, Vera, but I will soon enough. Then I might never let go."

"Good."

CHAPTER 31

It had taken a police escort and endless promises that she wouldn't leave Michael's building for her father to step out of the way and let her leave. Now that she was settled in, all she could do was watch the door and wait for Jay. Her instinct was to run to him and pull him close. That was hardly professional. Clearly inappropriate. Not something she would ever have considered doing. But wasn't that list getting longer since she'd met Jay?

Apparently he'd been thinking the same thing. The second he pushed through the glass doors to the lobby he jogged toward her and pulled her to him. His arms were around her, the kind of hug that permeated the skin and bones, straight down to the soul.

"I'm so sorry for what happened." He kissed her cheek as he spoke, trailing kisses all the way to her lips.

Michael cleared his throat and chuckled. "I'm not running that kind of establishment here."

"Sorry," Vera choked out as she hopped back and pressed the imaginary wrinkles out of her shirt.

"I need to talk to you both. Come on back to my office. I have an update." Michael's expression was too hard to read. It certainly didn't seem like good news. When they were sitting across from his desk she started to get the impression something was very wrong. "They haven't found any direct connection between your attacker and Daryl. The payment was made through some kind of wire transfer that isn't linked to Daryl in anyway. On an initial investigation the police don't see any kind of phone communication or digital connection between them either. Now it's early. They can work the case harder. But Daryl was released this morning. He claims he has no idea what happened and can't think of a reason why anyone would want to stop the work on Mary-Lee's case."

"He's lying." Jay stood up to make his case but Michael waved for him to sit down.

"Of course he is. But we don't know why and we don't know yet how to connect the two men."

Vera had an idea bolt through her. "Then let's figure out why he'd want to keep Mary-Lee in prison. Why wouldn't he want to have the case revisited?"

Michael nodded his agreement. "The police are working the other angle. This is our best shot to help. Take everything we know and see how we can connect that to Daryl."

Jay turned and looked out the window, clearly spinning through the choices. "If he hired someone to hurt Vera I want to crush him. Forget the courts. Forget what the police say. I want a crack at him."

"All right." Michael shrugged. "That would be the easiest option for me. Otherwise I'm going to have to suspend my caseload for the next three days and lock myself in this room dissecting a very old case. I'll have to call in my favors to experts. It'll be a lot of work. Or you can just go pummel the guy. End up in prison yourself. Solid plan."

"Jay, you came here for a chance. The best chance possible.

You worked through school, day and night. You've done everything to better your odds at helping your mother. I don't think it gets better than this." She squeezed his arm and gave him a warm promising smile. "I'm not going to visit you in prison."

"Yes you would." He let out a long sigh. "Fine. We do it the logical and legal way. But if he tries anything else, even comes close to hurting anyone I care about, I'm going to hunt him down."

"Wait." Michael stood abruptly and moved to the door, whispering something to the secretary. "Get them on the line now."

"Who?" Vera's heart thudded. Something seemed wrong.

"You just said if he hurts anyone else you care about. Your mother. This is a serious enough threat it could reach her in prison. If he wants the case left alone, getting rid of the current convicted person would certainly help his cause." His phone beeped, and he relayed the urgent message to someone from the prison. Michael insisted that she be put in isolated custody until the police settled their investigation into the assailant in Edenville. After he directed them to the detectives working the case, he hung up and leaned back in his chair.

"Thank you," Jay murmured. "I wouldn't have thought of that."

"Thinking is going to be all we do for a while. We need a war room. I'll have some food brought up and any other pertinent documents and evidence laid out. You two have done a great job of summarizing the case and looking for opportunities for a new trial. Now we change gears. We look for the reason Daryl is involved."

"We tried that." Jay was clearly feeling pessimistic. The will that had driven him this far had been challenged.

Michael gave a look filled with understanding. "I appreciate how much work you've put into this. But it's personal to you. We can offer expertise and perspective. Those two things can make all the difference."

"We can do this." Vera stood as if we every second would count. "Daryl crossed the wrong group of people."

CHAPTER 32

Piper stared at the white board in Michael's conference room as if it was speaking to her. "You guys did a great job on this." She followed the new timeline and notes that related specifically to Daryl. "I'm going with my gut, but I think your answer is here." She pointed to the notes about Susan Ikes. "This is Mary-Lee's best friend. She gives us a window into who Daryl really is. She didn't accept his advances. But if she had, where do you think that relationship would have gone? These are his true colors. Susan has nothing to gain from the truth. More to lose actually. It impacts her own reputation. If we believe what she said, then it's not too far a leap to assume there were other mistresses."

Michael took a few notes. "You're suggesting infidelity as a motive? Finding other women who were in his life at the time might be challenging. So much time has passed."

"We have his phone records," Jay pulled out the stack. "If he had a pattern, people he called regularly, maybe we can track them down."

Vera twisted her face up. "We should call his wife." She crossed her arms and looked ready to argue her point.

No one answered. Glances passed between them as they thought it over. Jay could see the value but there was little chance Piper and Michael would think that tactic would fly.

Michael broke first. "What would you ask her?"

Vera perked up. "We just lay it out for her. We have concerns about Daryl's involvement in Pauly's death."

Piper looked reluctant. "She'll have lawyered up after last night. She won't tell us anything."

"Maybe not." Vera shrugged. "But if somewhere in her mind there is the slightest bit of doubt, maybe she'll open up. It's worth a try."

"Who should call?" Piper asked, looking to Michael. "She's not going to want to talk to a lawyer."

"Vera should." Michael jutted his chin out in her direction. "She sounds young. Disarming. She's the victim. It might be compelling enough for her to connect with."

"I agree." Piper slid the phone over to her. "Just keep it short. Tell her who you are. Ask her if she's willing to talk."

Michael went through the documents he had. "Genevieve Stevens. Here's her number. It was your idea, and it's a good one."

She pursed her lips and dialed. Jay pulled his chair closer and put a hand on her thigh. "You've got this," he whispered.

"Hello?" The voice on the other end of the line was shaky, tired sounding.

"Genevieve, my name is Vera, do you have a minute to talk with me?"

"Vera?" she barked the words out. "What do you want? I don't have anything to say."

"I'm guessing you know what happened?" she licked her lips and clutched Jay's hand tightly. "I was attacked last night. The attacker named your husband as the man who hired him."

"He didn't." She bit the words out angrily. "Lies. You think I don't know my husband?"

Michael pumped his hands indicating she should slow down. Be calm.

"I'm sure you do know your husband. I'm not calling to accuse him of anything. I was pretty shaken up last night, and I just thought maybe you and I could talk."

"What would we have to talk about?"

"You're aware that Daryl was married to Mary-Lee and had a child years ago?" She held he breath.

"Of course I know that. I know the baby died, his wife poisoned the baby. Trust me he's told me all about it. We have children. He would never do anything to jeopardize his life with them. You can't imagine what kind of father he is. He came to every single appointment while I was pregnant with every one of our children. Their pediatric appointments, he was always there. That's why I know he would not hire some knife-wielding creep."

Piper scratched down a note and held it up so she could see. *Are they sick?*

"My father is the same way." Vera forced a smile. "He said he was a nervous wreck when I was born. Do your children go to the doctor often?"

"No, they are healthy kids. I know what you're implying. Daryl would never hurt our children. He paid thousands of dollars for extra genetic testing when they were born. He wanted to know they were healthy. What that woman did was disgusting. It takes a monster to want to hurt her own child. It impacted Daryl. It made him the father he is today."

"So you don't think he had anything to do with the hiring of the man who came to hurt me? There are no bank accounts he keeps separate or secret? Nothing you've found over time that has made you worry?"

"Bank accounts?" She huffed out the word. "I do all our

finances. I always have. Every penny is accounted for. Just like I told the police. We have all our home finances, the girls private school tuition, and the two thousand dollars a month he still sends to Mary-Lee. He takes care of her. Did you know that? What kind of man still sends money to the woman who murdered his child?"

Jay leaned forward, ready to argue but Michael gave him a look of warning. He drew in a deep breath and clenched his hands into fists.

Vera looked like a cartoon who just had a great idea, a lightbulb turning on over her head. "What did he have the children tested for?"

"Excuse me?"

"Your kids are young, there are an abundance of newborn screening tests now. They cover most issues. He insisted on further testing?"

"Yes, mostly with our first daughter. Because he was traumatized. That woman did that to him."

"What specifically were the kids tested for?"

"Why would that be important?" Her voice cracked suddenly. Jay could sense there were limits to her blind support. There was no way a man like Daryl had straightened his life out enough. Surely he'd given her a few reasons to question him.

"I'm sure it isn't," Vera began. "But it goes to his character. The lengths he's gone to make sure his children are healthy. I don't think that he's what the police are saying he is. But help me understand better."

"I don't know everything they were tested for off the top of my head, but it was genetic. I only remember the letters. One was PNA. But a certain one. Like there were many versions of that. The doctors didn't even want to do the testing because some things they were testing for were so rare. I've got all the paperwork. Daryl keeps it together. It's important to him."

"I understand."

"I have to go," she said quickly as a man's voice rang out behind her. "Don't call me anymore."

The line went dead and the room fell completely silent. Did they have something? Had this worked? So far every lead had only resulted in more questions.

"I need to make some calls about PNA. We need to know if it has anything to do with what happened to Pauly. Why was Daryl so concerned for his children? Did he know something?"

"How could he?" Piper asked circling the room as her mind seemed to circle around the facts. "How would he know his baby had something so serious and all the doctors all missed it? If he did know that something besides Mary-Lee caused Pauly's death, why not tell someone?"

Jay felt his stomach sour. The idea of his mother sitting in prison for something she didn't do while a man like Daryl had the answer all along was enough to send him into a blind rage. "He didn't want to be married to her anymore. That's obvious. What better way than to have her locked up for the rest of her life? Then he goes on looking like the victim."

Vera's hands were shaking as she ran them across her cheeks. "I think maybe that was Daryl in the background. Do you think he sounded upset?"

"He's going to know how upset I am." Jay stood and considered snatching the keys up and hopping in the car. He could be face to face with Daryl in a matter of hours.

"We have a lead," Piper said, pointing to the chair Jay had just hopped out of. "That means we work it. All of us."

"I can beat the answers out of him." Jay bit hard at the inside of his lip.

"A man like Daryl won't crack," Michael explained. "If he knew what killed Pauly and he's been hiding it for all these years, nothing we can do will get him to admit it. He has too much on the line. There is only one way to get him now, and that's with proof."

Jay could feel his blood thumping past his ear drums. "And if you don't find it?"

Michael set his jaw in anger. "Then I might take that ride with you and bring our bail money."

CHAPTER 33

"Thanks for taking my call Dr. Monteria. I know you're a busy woman." Michael leaned in to the phone. "It's a time sensitive matter."

"I just wrapped up in the lab. They told me you had called. I assumed it was important. I still owe you for the help you gave my brother-in-law last year. I'll do what I can for you."

"We need to know about PNA. It's a rare genetic disorder. The case I'm working on is decades old. An infant died and the courts ruled that it was due to antifreeze poisoning. We need to know if there might be a genetic disorder that could have caused the death instead."

"PNA is indeed very rare. It can be fatal, but only if left untreated. If well managed with intramuscular hydroxocobalamin, oral betaine, folinic acid, l-carnitine, and dietary protein modification, life expectancy is considered within normal range. Newborns are screened for it now, but decades ago we knew a lot less about it."

Michael looked pleased but Vera wouldn't allow herself to be hopeful. Not yet. There were still too many dots to connect. So much time had passed. But Michael drove farther down the path. "What would the symptoms be?"

"A general failure to thrive. Vomiting. Overall stomach trouble. It would get worse with the introduction of solid foods. Years ago an infant may not have been diagnosed at birth, but once the child was given solid foods the symptoms could not be overlooked. The body doesn't process nutrients correctly. In severe cases fluid can gather on the brain. That can cause lethargy."

Jay paced. "How about the antifreeze? None of this matters if it doesn't explain the blood work."

Dr. Monteria paused. "I'm checking that now. The 'A' in PNA stands for Acidemia. Essentially some foods are metabolized into acid. In a lab like ours we'd do adequate testing to ensure a higher level of ethanol or glycol in the blood could be sourced and then determine the reason for it. If you're talking about a doctor who isn't familiar with or looking for a genetic disorder, the results could certainly be misread as poisoning."

"Why wouldn't his other children have this? Why don't I?"

The question clearly threw the doctor off her game. She hadn't been warned the case was so personal. "I don't know your relationship to the child. However, those afflicted with this disorder are either lacking functional copies or adequate levels of important enzymes. Both parents have to have that genetic makeup to create this deficiency."

"What about DDA," Vera asked, forgetting to even introduce herself. "In the margins of one of the child's medical records, someone had written DDA with a question mark near it."

"Hmm," Dr. Monteria said. "They would have been on the right track, however the symptoms would not have been a complete match. PNA is a far more likely scenario. But if he'd been living with the disease for months something had to change to cause his death."

"He was in the hospital when he died." Michael pulled up those records. "They listed him as having acute malnutrition and dehydration. Likely from the vomiting. There is a note about flushing the body of the poison. They gave him a feeding tube and a diet high in protein and sodium. The notes indicated he was not responding to the diet and still seemed lethargic and undernourished. The day before his death they increased his volume of food."

"I'm not an expert in this field," the doctor qualified. "I haven't looked at a single thing related specifically to this patient."

"I won't hold you to anything you say today," Michael promised. "If we're on the right path I'll get you full access to the information for you to assess. Then you could perhaps consider testifying."

"I think you are on the right path," the doctor confirmed. "The increase in the volume of food likely put the child into a compromised situation leading to his death. For a child with PNA, more food means more toxic chemicals in the body. It can be treated and compensated for, but just loading him with more nutrients via a feeding tube likely resulted in his death."

Jay leaned back in his chair and ran his hands through his hair in exhaustion and relief. But he also wore the expression of someone who realized this was still only the beginning.

"Thank you, Lilly," Michael whispered, switching to her first name. "I've got some other calls to make but I'm going to send over all the records we have."

The doctor had one more request. "Are there tissue samples? If not, are both biological parents still living? The testing could be done on them to determine if their genetic makeup would be likely to result in PNA."

"They are both living," Michael reported with a smile. "One might be more willing than the other to be tested."

"I'm sure you can compel them." Lilly laughed. "Or maybe Betty can."

They disconnected the line and Vera couldn't help but let out a hoot. There was finally something to go on. Something that made sense. "This has to be it!"

Jay banged a hand down on the desk. "How did Daryl know? When did he find out?"

"That's the piece we have to sort out," Michael agreed. "There is usually one sure fire way to do that."

"Which is?" Vera asked, realizing how much she intended to learn this summer and how much she'd already surpassed her expectation.

"Follow the money. There has to be some link to Daryl finding out about the PNA and money."

Vera scanned her mind, remembering that his new wife had claimed she could account for all their money except what Daryl sent to Mary-Lee every month.

"Did your mother confirm that Daryl still sends her money every month? What would she do with two thousand dollars a month in prison? Plus, when Daryl was playing martyr he would have mentioned that he still sends that money."

Michael snapped his fingers. "Great point. There is no way she's getting two thousand a month from him. She wouldn't have use for that much where she is. We need to find out where that money is really going."

"Follow the money," Jay agreed.

CHAPTER 34

This was the hardest thing Jay had ever done. His hand was balled into a fist, and he knew how to knock on a door but for some reason he couldn't. After a long moment of standing there, Vera finally did.

The small cottage was by the sea. It was decorated with shells and painted a pale ocean blue. They'd gotten the address just that morning, and it took them no time to decide to come in person. This house was paid for every month with Daryl's money. There was no indication of why. So they were here to find out.

"Can I help you?" There was a woman standing in the doorway, her hair pinned up. Kind brown eyes and a welcoming smile were more than Jay had expected.

"My name is Jay, this is Vera. We wanted to talk to you for a little bit."

"About Jesus?" she asked, looking them up and down.

"No," he laughed and shook his head, "about Daryl Stevens."

Her tiny smile faded away. "What about him?"

"He pays for this property, right?" Vera asked, trying to sound casual. "We have some questions about why he does that."

"Are you from the IRS?"

"I think people from the IRS dress better than us," Vera joked. "We know Daryl. He was married to Jay's mother. We're wondering how you know him."

"We were together many years ago. A lifetime ago."

"But he pays for you to still live here?" Jay looked around the living room behind her. It was quaint and quiet. Though there was something in the corner of the room that caught his eye. An IV machine. "Do you live here alone?"

"My son lives with me. But I'm not sure I can answer your questions. Daryl is a private man, and I don't want to discuss his business. Can't you ask him?"

Vera apparently decided there was no time to dance around it. "The last time I asked him questions he sent a man with a knife to shut me up. You can see why I would much rather deal with someone like you. A mom. A woman who clearly lives a peaceful life. Please, we won't take up much of your time."

"I don't particularly want a man with a knife coming after me either." The woman folded her arms across her chest. But her words were telling. She hadn't denied that Daryl was that kind of man. She was only asserting she didn't intend to deal with the fallout for talking.

"We can make sure that doesn't happen, as long as we work together," Jay pleaded with a look of desperation. "My mother is in prison for something I don't think she did. If there is anything you can tell us, please do."

"What is she in prison for?" She took a small step back and braced herself.

"For killing their child. But she didn't. We believe he was sick. We also believe Daryl knew."

"PNA?" She gasped.

Jay felt his chest explode with furious fireworks. His ears rattled. Everything stood still.

Vera finally asked. "How did you know that?"

"You might as well come in," the woman said, stepping aside. "I guess we'll have a lot to talk about." She sighed and gestured toward the couch. "My name is Samantha Burge."

"Thank you, Samantha," Vera said genuinely. Jay could still not find the words. "You may be exactly what we've been waiting for."

"I may be what you've been looking for, but we're what Daryl has been trying to hide for decades. It's worked until now. I've always kind of wondered when someone would come knocking here."

"Why would Daryl want to hide you?" Vera asked, one hand clutching Jay's knee as they sat down. She needed him to know she was there. That the earth was still spinning on its axis.

"I'm thirty-six."

"Okay?"

"My son is twenty. Daryl is his father."

"You were fifteen when you were together?" Vera scrambled to put it into a story that could make sense. "But Daryl wasn't. He was in his late twenties."

"Right."

"So he's kept you hidden away so no one knew he'd had a child with an underage girl?" Vera looked rightfully disgusted.

"It started that way. But he promised me that someday it wouldn't matter. Once I was old enough we could be together. I believed him. Then I had Skyler and everything changed. He was sick. It took a lot of testing but they diagnosed him with PNA. The treatment was expensive, and Daryl told me it would be better if we weren't married or living together because then the government could pay for everything. I believed that too. He would come out to Oklahoma and visit us as often as he could, but he told me his office was in North Carolina and it was important for him to be there."

"Daryl knew he had a child with PNA?" Jay finally put the words he wanted together. "When did he know?"

"When Skylar was diagnosed. He was six months old. It was October of that year."

Jay and Vera looked at each other as they did the math. Vera was the first to put the timeline together. "Two months after your mother was convicted."

Jay could hardly grasp the truth. "He had two children within months of each other. Pauly dies and then he finds out his second child has a genetic disorder that could have accounted for the symptoms and death of his first child."

Vera whispered hoarsely. "And he never said a thing. He let your mother sit in prison rather than admit he had done something illegal and immoral by having a child with Samantha. He could have even pretended to stumble upon the answer. Instead he said nothing."

"I didn't know," Samantha gasped out. "I had nothing to do with it."

Jay felt an odd calm come over him. "Everyone take a breath. This is a lot to take in. Samantha, are you comfortable going on the record with what you've told us today?"

"I've been taking his money." She folded her hands in her lap. "But this month he said I'd have to hold the money and give it to someone else. A man was going to come pick it up."

"Could you identity the man?" Vera fumbled for her cell phone and scrolled frantically for a picture.

"No," Jay said, having a moment of clarity. "Let her identify him in a police lineup. Let's do this the right way."

"He had a birthmark over his eyebrow," Samantha reported. Vera let out a tiny gasp then choked back her emotions.

"I didn't know what it was for, and I didn't know about your mother. You don't know what kind of man Daryl is. He moved us here about eleven years ago because he thought it would be cheaper, paying for a little property like this and my son getting treatment at a research hospital that provides care for free. Before that I was just a spot on his map. A place he traveled to for work and then forgot about. I didn't know until years later he was married, and I never knew he lost a child."

"But you'll testify he knew the child you share had PNA? You'll identify the man you gave the money to on Daryl's orders?" Jay could feel his chest rising and falling with each breath, but the oxygen barely felt like it was reaching his brain.

"What will happen to my son?" Samantha gulped and wiped away a stray tear from her cheek. "The money that Daryl sends, it's everything to us. My son needs treatments and I can't work full time."

"I don't know the answer to that," Jay admitted. "All I know is my mother has sat in prison for decades with the label of child killer. I've grown up without her. You can't imagine what she's gone through."

"I can't," Samantha whispered. "I can't imagine. I'll talk to whoever you want. But if he's willing to send someone after you to keep you quiet, imagine what he'd do to me. To our son. He does not want the world knowing I was fifteen years old when we were together. He doesn't want his wife knowing he still pays me. You'll back him into a corner, and you can't do that with a man like Daryl. He acts so proper. He makes the world think he's a nice guy."

"We know he isn't." Vera plucked her cell phone from her bag. "I need to make some phone calls. I know some people who can help." She excused herself and stepped out the front door, already talking to Michael.

"This isn't how I pictured it," Jay admitted, looking around the little cottage and then back to Samantha.

"Pictured what?"

"The day I found something that would set my mother free, I

didn't think it would look like this. I knew it would feel like this though. I'd know when it cracked wide open."

"I hope you don't think I'm the answer to all your prayers."

"Why not?"

"My track record says the odds aren't in my favor. If I'm what you're hanging your hope on, you might want to keep looking."

"Samantha," Jay began as he reached across and took her hand. "I know exactly what you mean, but our luck is about to change."

CHAPTER 35

"I just want to see him in cuffs." Jay stood outside the courthouse, waiting to catch a glimpse. "I need to see his face when they read the charges against him."

"It won't be nearly as good as when your mother walks free." Michael slapped a hand to his shoulder. "Samantha did an amazing job identifying the man she paid on Daryl's behalf as the same man who attacked Vera. The rest of the charges are murky. There are limitations on how many years passed in reference to his relationship with Samantha and her age at the time. But hiring a hit man, that will keep him locked up for a long time."

Vera bit at her bottom lip. "I just keep thinking about his kids and his wife. I know what he did was wrong. I know he's a terrible person. But their lives are going to be put under a microscope now. Everything is going to be uprooted."

"The wife's sister gave a statement to police that Daryl had a temper and had on at least two occasions struck his wife and left her with bruises. You may have saved her life. A man like Daryl has this vision of what he's supposed to be. Business mogul. Family man. Public figure. But those things don't line up with who he really is. He wants to run around and cheat. He wants to bury secrets. Those things collide, and he lashes out. It may never have caught up with him if it weren't for you two."

"How long until she's out?" Jay felt like a child counting down the days until Christmas, bugging all the grown ups every chance he got. But the answer was fluid. It had changed. Michael was doing everything necessary, but it wasn't only a matter of telling a judge they'd gotten it wrong. There was a process. There were test results to wait for.

"We're making good progress." Michael was noncommittal.

"How did she seem last time you talked to her? Is she asking about this as often as I am?" He let out a little chuckle, but Michael didn't change his expression.

"It's very normal for someone in her position to be hesitant. Hope is a difficult thing to hold onto in prison, especially in her circumstances. We're getting there. The results of the samples provided to the lab were positive for PNA. It won't take long now. You just start planning for what to do when she comes homes."

"Betty said she could stay in the apartment above the restaurant for a while. I'm going to work there and help out so we can be close."

"She's going to need a lot of support," Vera chimed in. "Once we go back to school you might need to look for other options for her. Something with lots of resources."

"I'm done with school." Jay hadn't given it much thought. Of course he wasn't going back to the law school. It wasn't his passion. He was barely getting by anyway. Now that he had hope for his mother's freedom there was nothing else he could learn in the classroom that would make a difference.

"You're not?" Vera's voice was high and in that moment he realized he'd overlooked that one detail. She might care. Their colleges weren't all that far from each other and of course she assumed that when they went back, maybe they'd go back together.

"I can't afford to pay to fail all the time. I'm going to have my mother back in my life, and I want to be there for her. I won't need a law degree."

Michael leaned in and lowered his voice. "You probably weren't going to get it anyway."

"You could change your major." Vera looked winded by the whole idea. "You can't just hang around Edenville forever."

"My favorite girl is from here," he teased. "That's enough to make me want to do more than just visit."

"The only problem is I won't be here."

Michael was cracking himself up. "I think he might have been talking about Betty."

"Here comes Daryl," Jay said, straightening to his full height. Two officers escorted him into the building but not before Jay could make eye contact and get the last word in.

Vera slid her hand into his. "Looks like he's been through the ringer." She was right. Gone was the man they'd met in his downtown office. His orange jumpsuit and unkempt hair was nothing compared to the bewildered look in his eyes. Like an animal whose foot was snagged in a trap. Jay shoved himself forward a step so that Daryl would have no choice but to look his way. And when he did Jay got exactly what he wanted. Daryl's face flickered abruptly through confusion, to recognition, to defeat.

"Got what you came for?" Michael asked, fishing out his car keys and nodding in the direction of the parking lot.

"Yeah." Jay looped his arm over Vera's shoulder and kissed her sweet-smelling hair. "I've almost got everything I need."

CHAPTER 36

It wasn't like he imagined. There was no big crowd standing outside the prison when his mother walked out. She didn't even seem all that happy. More shocked. Skittish. Michael had been good enough to connect them with a counselor who specialized in acclimating after a long prison sentence.

What had been more impactful was speaking with Jedda. He was member of the family apparently, in the way that he was not really related but had been absorbed in like water to a sponge. Jedda had served time in prison for a crime he did commit, but with the help and support of everyone he was able to find his place in the world again. His advice had been clear: Don't expect too much.

Jay had been trying that. Low expectations. His mother didn't have to be overjoyed. She could still be sad. She could still be angry. Confused. Telling her the news of Daryl's involvement had rocked her. Someone she thought she knew was a stranger. Someone she thought she could trust betrayed her, and it cost her years of her life. Years that couldn't be reclaimed.

Any fantasy Jay had of becoming instantly connected to his

mother and healing all the pain that had befallen them evaporated quickly. That wasn't a fairytale. She didn't know him. He didn't know her.

"Mary-Lee," Betty sang as she put a cup of hot tea down in front of her. "You are welcome to stay here as long as you like. That room you are in has housed folks from all walks of life, and I'm nearly convinced it's magic at this point."

"And I'll be here working at the restaurant." Jay put a hand over hers. "I'll be close by."

"No," Mary-Lee said, shaking her head. "You're going up north."

"I'm not going back to school. I don't want to be a lawyer. I never really did. I can be here with you."

"I don't think you should be here with me," Mary-Lee admitted. "I don't know who I am yet. I'm not ready to be your mother. Not all at once. Not up close."

The revelation, though he'd already felt it, still stung. "I'm not trying to crowd you. I can give you space."

"Guilt is a powerful thing." Mary-Lee hung her head.

"But you are innocent." Jay heard the urgency in his voice, but he couldn't tamp it down.

"Innocent of a crime but not completely innocent as a person. I want to know you. I love you. But I am not ready to be what you need. And being with you every day, you waiting for me to turn into something, the guilt will kill me."

Jay opened his mouth to argue but couldn't muster the words. Even if he won, he'd lose in the long run.

"Vera hasn't left yet," Betty reported from behind her own mug of coffee. "I'm certain there would be a job for you somewhere near her. You've both been through so much this summer. Surely you aren't ready for that to be over."

"It's not over. We decided to make it work long distance." Jay swirled the spoon in his coffee mug and thought of Vera. She'd been so kind about his decision. So committed to keeping what they had alive even if it was hard.

"I'm the one you should have a long distance relationship with." His mother reached up and touched his cheek. "You and I can talk on the phone, ease back into this life of ours. What you have with her, it's a fire you should keep stoked."

"You'll be all right?" Jay asked, wondering how she could possibly manage without him now that they had a chance to be together.

"You'll come back next summer? Maybe the holidays too?"

"Of course."

Betty shared her warm smile with them. "She won't be alone. We're good at this kind of stuff around here."

"Go catch that girl. Don't let her leave. I'm not sure I'd be here if it wasn't for her."

Jay hopped to his feet and kissed his mother's cheek and then Betty's. "I'll call you when we get there."

"Please do."

As he raced out the door he heard Betty whisper to his mother. "That couldn't have been easy for you."

His mother replied sweetly. "I'll do anything for my son. He's done everything for me."

She was still there, packing up the pickup truck as he pulled in, and relief washed over him. "Vera, wait." He breathlessly spilled from the car and charged over to her. "I'm coming with you."

"What?" She looked like he had run up and pushed a pie into her face. "You're staying here with your mother."

"She told me to go. I know Betty and everyone else can take good care of her. I think she and I need time to build something and we might do better if I'm not hovering over her, worried every two seconds if she's all right. Plus …"

"Plus what?" Her eyes were welling with hopeful tears.

"Plus I love you. I want to be there when you conquer the world. I'll be the guy who holds your purse and gets your coffee."

"Just be the guy who loves me." She pulled him in for a kiss. "That's all I want."

The screen door squeaked open and her father stepped out. "It's about time." He shook the truck keys up and then tossed them to Jay. "Drive safe. Call when you get there."

"You're fine not driving me to college?" Vera scrutinized his expression.

"No, I'm not fine. I haven't been fine since the first day you learned to walk and toddled out of my arms. But that's my problem. How hard it is to let you go shouldn't be a reason to make you suffer. Jay's a good man. If he's smart enough to realize how amazing it is to have you in his life, then I say let him drive."

Vera drew in a steadying breath, but it was hopeless. She'd broken down into tears. Sobs. "I'll be home for Thanksgiving."

"Odds are I'll drive up there in a few weeks anyway and make some lame excuse to see you."

"Good," she murmured as she raced up to hug him.

"There's a cooler full of food from Betty in the cab of the truck. Full tank of gas. Brand new belt on it. You should be fine." He clutched her tightly and spoke into her hair. "You should be fine."

"I will be. You've always made sure of that."

Jay didn't have to wonder anymore what it might be like to love that deeply. He understood it now. When Vera finally jumped into the passenger seat of the truck and he threw it into gear, it felt like the starting line of a long race. The beginning of what he had been holding his breath and waiting for.

"You sure about this?" he asked as she blew a kiss to her father.

"No." She sighed and laced her fingers with his. "But I am sure about us."

The End

ALSO BY DANIELLE STEWART

Piper Anderson Series:

Book 1: Chasing Justice

Book 2: Cutting Ties

Book 3: Changing Fate

Book 4: Finding Freedom

Book 5: Settling Scores

Book 6: Battling Destiny

Book 7: Unearthing Truth

Book 8: Defending Innocence

Piper Anderson Bonus Material:

Chris & Sydney Collection – Choosing Christmas & Saving Love

Betty's Journal - Bonus Material (suggested to be read after Book 4 to avoid spoilers)

Edenville Series – A Piper Anderson Spin Off:

Book 1: Flowers in the Snow

Book 2: Kiss in the Wind

Book 3: Stars in a Bottle

Book 4: Fire in the Heart

Piper Anderson Legacy Mystery Series:

Book 1: Three Seconds To Rush

Book 2: Just for a Heartbeat

Book 3: Not Just an Echo

The Clover Series:

Hearts of Clover - Novella & Book 2: (Half My Heart & Change My Heart)

Book 3: All My Heart

Over the Edge Series:

Book 1: Facing Home

Book 2: Crashing Down

Midnight Magic Series:

Amelia

Rough Waters Series:

Book 1: The Goodbye Storm

Book 2: The Runaway Storm

Book 3: The Rising Storm

Stand Alones:

Running From Shadows

Yours for the Taking

****

Multi-Author Series including books by Danielle Stewart

All are stand alone reads and can be enjoyed in any order.

Indigo Bay Series:
A multi-author sweet romance series

Sweet Dreams - Stacy Claflin
Sweet Matchmaker - Jean Oram
Sweet Sunrise - Kay Correll
Sweet Illusions - Jeanette Lewis
Sweet Regrets - Jennifer Peel
Sweet Rendezvous - Danielle Stewart

Short Holiday Stories in Indigo Bay:
A multi-author sweet romance series

Sweet Holiday Wishes - Melissa McClone
Sweet Holiday Surprise - Jean Oram
Sweet Holiday Memories - Kay Correll
Sweet Holiday Traditions - Danielle Stewart

Return to Christmas Falls Series:
A multi-author sweet romance series

Homecoming in Christmas Falls: Ciara Knight
Honeymoon for One in Christmas Falls: Jennifer Peel
Once Again in Christmas Falls: Becky Monson
Rumor has it in Christmas Falls: Melinda Curtis
Forever Yours in Christmas Falls: Susan Hatler
Love Notes in Christmas Falls: Beth Labonte
Finding the Truth in Christmas Falls: Danielle Stewart

****

BOOKS IN THE BARRINGTON BILLIONAIRE SYNCHRONIZED WORLD

By Ruth Cardello:

Always Mine

Stolen Kisses

Trade It All

Let It Burn

More Than Love

By Jeannette Winters:

One White Lie

Table For Two

You & Me Make Three

Virgin For The Fourth Time

His For Five Nights

After Six

Seven Guilty Pleasures

By Danielle Stewart:

Fierce Love

Wild Eyes

Crazy Nights

Loyal Hearts

Untamed Devotion

Stormy Attraction

Foolish Temptations

You can now download all Barrington Billionaire books by Danielle Stewart in a "Sweet" version. Enjoy the clean and wholesome version, same story without the spice. If you prefer the hotter version be sure to download the original. <u>The Sweet version still contains adult situations and relationships.</u>

Fierce Love - Sweet Version

Wild Eyes - Sweet Version

Crazy Nights - Sweet Version

Loyal Hearts - Sweet Version

Untamed Devotion - Sweet Version

Stormy Attraction - Sweet Version - Coming Soon

Foolish Temptations - Sweet Version - Coming Soon

NEWSLETTER SIGN-UP

If you'd like to stay up to date on the latest Danielle Stewart news visit www.authordaniellestewart.com and sign up for my newsletter.

One random newsletter subscriber will be chosen every month this year. The chosen subscriber will receive a $25 eGift Card! Sign up today.

AUTHOR CONTACT INFORMATION

Website: AuthorDanielleStewart.com
Email: AuthorDanielleStewart@Gmail.com
Facebook: facebook.com/AuthorDanielleStewart
Twitter: @DStewartAuthor